THE UNION

III

The Finale

CHAPTER ONE

When the shot rang out, Mox's initial instinct was to lunge for Brandi. Again, she screamed, "Daddy!" and raced down the steps.

"Brandi, get down!"

The bullet struck Jennifer in the middle of her forehead—she was stretched across the living room floor—blood, seeping from the small dimple in her skull. Priscilla's face was flushed with gloom as she clasped the handle of the murder weapon. Her soaking eyes dropped to the corpse; one deep breath, then another.

"Priscilla, let's go!" Mox yelled. He held Brandi in his arms at the front door.

Priscilla looked up. The fear she saw in Brandi's eyes was heart wrenching. Her only seed—a child, subject to the jagged realities of a world she had never asked to be birthed into. A beautiful baby girl, who was unconscious to life's rights and wrongs, oblivious to decision making, but included in every decision made.

This wasn't the life for a child. This wasn't life for anyone.

She gripped the pistol tighter and the tears came down faster. A sour, dreaded feeling bubbled at the base of her stomach. Priscilla murmured. "Do you really love me, Mox?" Silence lingered in the gunpowder-filled air, and her eyes were locked on Mox's face. "Do you love your daughter?" Her arm was moving upward, and the gun was still in her hand.

"Priscilla, put the gun down and let's go."

The small droplets continued to cascade down her cheeks. "I gave you everything, Mox." She inched her pointer finger around the trigger.

"What's left to give?" Her voice was low and barely audible.

Mox stood in silence. His focus was keyed on Priscilla's trigger finger. Quickly, he moved to her eyes. They were riddled with agony and defeat, stress and despair. He saw in them the beautiful young lady he had met years back. She was still there—just fighting to be released; struggling for a chance to be loved.

"Don't do this, Priscilla. You know I love you. I've never in my life loved a woman the way I love you. Look..." He took a step towards her, Brandi clutched in the fold of his arms. "Look at our daughter."

"Stop lyin' to me, Mox!" Her voice gained volume. She was less than ten feet away with the gun pointed at his head.

Mox glanced down at Jennifer spread across the floor. The look on her face was sickening. He raised his head, and with his good eye, he peered down the barrel of the loaded handgun. "In about five minutes," he whispered. "This whole spot gon' be surrounded wit' police, and ain't no way I'm lettin' them muthafuckas take me back to that hell... so, either you shoot me right now, or put that fuckin' gun down and bring yo' ass on."

Minutes later...

"Brandi, make sure you have your seatbelt on." Priscilla rushed to start the car. She jammed the key into the ignition. "Where we goin?" she asked, turning to Mox.

For the first time in his life, Mox didn't have a plan. He hadn't had time to think this one through. "I don't know, but we gotta get the fuck outta here. Now."

Priscilla adjusted the rearview and put the car in gear. She took one more glance at Mox, smiled, and then mashed on the gas pedal.

"Damnit Six, we fucked up!" Tyrell slammed his fist on the table.

"Nah nigga... *you* fucked up. *You* gave the order."

Tyrell snatched a chair from underneath the table, sat down, and placed both hands on his head. "I don't believe this shit, fuck!"

The decision he made to have Leo killed turned out to be the wrong one, and now the burden of his death weighed solely upon his shoulders. Trying to include Six was a physiological move, but truthfully, he knew it was his doing and his doing alone.

"These are the muthafuckas you lookin' for, champ?" Boom Bam, an ex-football player turned hood legend, came from the back room and dropped a piece of paper on the table in front of Tyrell. They were in his apartment. He was Tyrell's best worker. "They definitely ain't from around here," he said.

Tyrell picked the paper up and stared at the two faces. "Is it them, Six?"

"Yup," six nodded. "That's them muhfuckas right there. I remember those faces anywhere."

"What the fuck these two white boys doin' in the hood, and who the fuck are they?" Tyrell was baffled. "Boom Bam, you can't find out who these dudes are?"

In college, Boom Bam was a computer expert, so in the hood he used his talents to support his lifestyle. He had the ability to hack into anything that could be hacked, and Tyrell summoned his expertise to get the video footage from the cameras set up in the lobby of the building. The task had been completed in a matter of minutes.

"Already done, champ." He dropped another piece of paper on the table. "This is serious business right here, y'all ready for this typea shit?"

Tyrell read the printout and then angrily crumbled the paper in his hands. "I don't give a fuck if that nigga name is John Gotti... they took somebody close to me. I'ma make 'em pay for that shit. I put that on everything." His thoughts drifted back to the last time he saw his cousin, Dana. It was equivalent to traveling down an empty passageway—one that had been avoided for specific reasons.

His grip tightened and he crushed the paper. He bit down on his back teeth and clenched his jaws. Measure for measure—eye for an eye, it was the only way. Losing a loved one—an extremely close loved one, birthed an animal not even Tyrell could contain. His initial introduction to the streets was money oriented, but now—now murder was becoming habitual, and his sensibility to love and human life had lessened.

Boom Bam and Six stood in the kitchen watching Tyrell as he went through his motions.

"I knew this lil' nigga was a bug-out." Boom Bam looked at Six. "He gon' get you killed."

Six was fearless, but he wasn't stupid. He acknowledged that the odds were beyond evenly matched. In fact, there were no odds according to him. *How could two young dudes from the projects wage war against a mafia crime family?*

"I think you need to take some time wit' this one... think it over a lil' bit." he said.

Tyrell looked up. "You think *I* need to take some time? *I* huh, what the fuck happened to *we*? It was just *we* this, *we* that... what happened to that shit, Six?"

Six didn't think he would catch it, but Tyrell was sharper than what most people assumed.

"I'm sayin', I—"

"You what?" When Tyrell stood up, Six got tongue-tied.

"I—"

"That's what I thought. Don't bitch up on me now, Six. It's crunch time, baby."

"I ain't bitchin' up, Rell. I'm jus' sayin'... we need to come up wit' a plan if we goin' at these dudes. We gotta use our brains on this one."

Tyrell reached into his pants and pulled his gun out. He held it in his palm while looking at Six. "You don't need brains when you got bullets, Six." He cocked the weapon and passed the barrel under his nose. Inhaling, he stared at Six and said, "Either you wit' me or you against me, and if you against me... you a dead man walkin'."

A shiver flowed through Six's body. He knew if it came to it, Tyrell wouldn't hesitate to kill him. He'd seen it done—he'd been a part of it. A choice had to be made, and time was more precious than a newborn baby.

Boom Bam's doorbell rang and they all looked at each other.

"Go see who it is, Boom..."

He walked to the door, put his eye to the peephole, and then looked back at Tyrell and Six. "It's the lil' nigga, O who used to stay in the hood. He prolly wanna cop."

Tyrell tucked his gun and then fixed his shirt over it. "Let 'em in."

When the door opened, a five feet tall young kid with a protruding belly, blue jeans, and a hoodie entered the apartment.

"Whaddup, Boom? I need five hunit soft." The kid reached into his jeans and came out with a wad of bills. He looked up at Tyrell and Six, and then took a seat on Boom Bam's sofa.

Tyrell caught a glimpse of the kid's face when he pulled his hoody back. "Yo, Omar, what the fuck you doin?"

"Oh shit... Rell... wassup?" Omar got up from the couch and walked over to Tyrell. "I aint even know that was you. Boom keep it mad dark in here, you can't see shit."

Tyrell hadn't seen Omar in years—since his mother had been sober and held the responsibility of caring for a few neighborhood kids. Back then, they played together, ate together and shared the same couch when it was nap time in the Michaels' house. And now, it looked like they were in the same line of business—the coke game.

"You hustlin' now, huh?" Tyrell smirked and his attention went to the pile of money Omar had laid out on the coffee table. If he was coming to buy five hundred grams at thirty dollars each, then it had to be at least $15,000 on the table.

Boom Bam appeared from the shadows holding a beat up Nike shoebox. He took a seat in his old, ragged, wooden rocking chair that was opposite of where Omar sat. He put the box on the table. "Y'all know each other?" he asked.

"Yeah, we know each other." Tyrell replied. "My mother use to watch this nigga. We practically grew up together... Yo, Omar how your moms doin'?"

"She's dead." he said, without a flinch.

"Damn, son. My condolences to you and the family. Where you at now?"

Omar cut his eye at Tyrell. "Homey, you askin' alotta questions, wassup wit' that?"

"Fuck you mean, wassup wit that?"

"You heard me, nigga." Omar stepped back and went to reach in his hoody, but Boom Bam jumped to his feet and got between the two young men.

"Y'all niggas chill the fuck out. This is my shit!" he growled.

Omar kept his hand in the front pocket of his hoody, "Who this nigga think he is, Boom?"

"Omar, sit yo' ass down." Boom Bam lightly shoved him towards the sofa. "Cool off, nigga." He turned to Tyrell. "Why you always startin' shit?"

Tyrell smiled and let out a slight chuckle. "You right, Boom. My bad."

Being the mediator, Boom Bam diffused the situation before it became hostile. He couldn't understand the mentality of today's youth because he'd grown up in a different era—an era where you fought your problems out if it came to it. But this was the norm now. He'd been watching kids kill kids for the past ten years, and it was becoming an epidemic.

"Y'all fuckin' retarded. I truly believe it's an entire generation of crack babies, and all y'all doin' is knockin' each other off." Boom Bam shook his head and then sat back in his chair. "That money right, O?"

"My money always right, Boom. You know that..." Omar paused and turned to Tyrell. "Wassup wit' your man, he good?"

Tyrell kept a straight face and held his composure, but what he really wanted to do was shove his gun down this bitchassnigga's throat and make him apologize for his rude behavior. But he was easy. He sat back and played the fool as expected.

Boom Bam picked up a half-smoked cigarette from the ashtray and lit it. "He cool." he answered, letting the smoke filter through his nostrils. He pulled a digital scale out the box along with a ziplock bag filled with cocaine rocks. While they conducted their business Tyrell and Six acted as if they were invisible, but they heard everything that was being said.

"Yooo," Omar was putting $1,000 stacks together and placing them to the side. "I ran into that nigga... umm..." He couldn't remember the name. "That big nigga that use to play football from out here, I think his last name is Davis or some shit like that."

"Who, Cleo?" Boom Bam questioned.

"Yeeaahh, that nigga. I bumped into son down in SC. He was doin' his numbers. I think that nigga on the run for somethin' though... he be mad nervous n' shit."

"Word?" Boom Bam brushed it off and never thought twice about it. He knew what Cleo was on the run for—shit, the whole hood knew why Cleo was on the run, but what Boom Bam didn't know was that Tyrell was involved.

After he weighed out the product and they made the exchange, Omar went on his way, but before he left, he said something slick. "Yo, Rell..." He was halfway out the door. "You was never a tough guy. Don't try to be one now. Boom, I'll see you on the next trip."

Tyrell got up and reached for his gun, but Boom Bam stopped him.

"Chill, Rell... he'll be back."

CHAPTER TWO

A delicate mist mixed with light flurries descended from the darkened sky as headlights from passing vehicles on the expressway served as extra light on the vacant streets. Tricia pranced up and down the strip in her wig, fake fur, tight skirt and four-inch heels, awaiting the arrival of a potential trick. A burning cigarette sat between her index and middle finger, while her eyes followed the dark grey Mercedes Benz that slowly passed.

"Get yo' skinny ass off the strip!" the passenger yelled.

"Fuck you, bitchassnigga!" The Benz pulled away from the curb and Tricia plucked the cigarette in the street. "Ol' broke ass nigga," she mumbled, checking the watch on her wrist. Headlights from a black Audi pulling into the parking lot forced her to shield her eyes, but she was adamant on seeing who the driver was. When she noticed it was a female, she sucked her teeth, rolled her eyes, and sashayed back into the lobby of the motel.

"Why did you tell me to get off at this exit, Mox?" Priscilla questioned as she tried to find a space to park.

"Because we hot, Priscilla. Since you and your little friend back there wanna do secret missions n' shit... this is what we gotta do."

Priscilla badly wanted to snap and curse Mox out, but she remembered Brandi was in the back seat. "Whatever you say, Mox." She mumbled, put the car in park and they exited the vehicle and entered the motel lobby.

The poignant aroma of badly cooked food filled the cramped lobby space causing Mox and Priscilla to turn up their nose. "Damn, it stinks in here." Mox complained.

Tricia stared at the couple as she sat in a chair off in the corner. "Hey Daddy." she said, smiling hard.

Mox heard her, but he ignored her.

Priscilla heard her and replied. "Bitch, you blind?"

"What?" Tricia stood up. She and Priscilla were almost the same size and height.

Priscilla let go of Brandi's hand and took a step forward. "You heard me, bitch. Are you blind?"

A sharp clicking sound caught Priscilla's attention. "Naw, but I bet you bleed." Tricia clutched an old school box-cutter in her right hand. She kept it low, but Mox saw it and stepped between them.

"Fuck is wrong wit' you?" he snatched the skinny prostitute by her weave and shoved her into the corner.

"Hey!" The attendant behind the glass yelled. "No fighting! I will call cops!" he shouted in his heavy foreign accent.

Tricia bounced against the hard plastic window and the razor fell from her grasp and hit the floor. She fixed her wig and skirt and bent down to pick up her weapon.

"You bedda get that bitch before I cut her."

"Try it, bitch. I dare you." Priscilla replied. She had her finger wrapped around the trigger of the gun in her pocket. After she was cut the first time, she vowed to never let it happen again.

"Priscilla!" Mox yelled. He felt Tricia take a step towards him, so he turned around. "Get your stupid ass outta here before you fuck around and get hurt."

Tricia mumbled a few words and then slithered out the front entrance, but kept an eye on Priscilla the whole time.

"Can we get a room, please?" Mox asked the attendant.

He stared at the couple with his dark eyes and then looked down at Brandi.

"How long?"

"One night."

"Forty dollars for the short stay, seventy-five for the night."

Mox turned to Priscilla. "You got money?"

"No."

He turned back to the attendant. "Hold on, I'll be right back." Mox breezed by Brandi and Priscilla and walked out to the parking lot. "Fuck!" He cursed himself as he headed back to the car. The burden of being financially unstable was eating away at his conscience, and he had no clue how he could make things right. He hit the unlock button on the car keys and searched through the vehicle for any loose bills that may have been lying around. "It gotta be somethin' in here." he said aloud.

After rummaging through the entire interior of the car and finding nothing, Mox popped the trunk and prayed for a miracle. He dug through a black bag that was full of Priscilla's clothes. As he continued to come up empty handed, he tossed garment after garment back into the trunk and his frustration grew more intense. He glanced over his shoulder and saw Priscilla and Brandi looking out at him from inside the motel lobby.

He started to say prayer as he pulled out the last pair of Priscilla's jeans, but he felt something in her left pocket. He reached in and came out holding two $100 bills. Mox shoved the remaining clothes back into the bag, slammed the trunk and kissed the money up to the sky as he walked towards the lobby. "Here," He said, pushing a hundred dollar bill through the hole in the glass. "One night please."

"Where'd you get that money from?" Priscilla asked.

"Mommy..." Brandi was crisscrossing her legs and she looked very agitated. "I gotta use the bathroom."

"Yo, can you speed that process up a lil' bit? My daughter gotta use the bathroom." Mox said.

The attendant stared at Mox from behind the glass. He picked his fork up, dug in his plate and ate a mouthful of food. After wiping the side of his mouth with a napkin, he said. "ID"

"Gimme your ID, Priscilla."

"I don't have my ID, Mox... I don't have anything. We left everything back there... and I asked you where'd you get that money."

"Shit!" Mox was heated. "Do it matter where I got the money from Priscilla, huh? This is it... this is all the fuckin' money we got right here. This one, one hundred dollar bill." He shook his head and paced the tight area. "I can't believe this shit."

"ID please. No ID, no room." The attendant said.

Mox approached the glass again. "Look man..." he said. "I'm in a fucked up situation as you can see. I really need this room. How 'bout I throw a extra $25 on it and you jus' pass me those keys?"

The attendant didn't say a word he just looked at Mox with a grin on his face. Seconds later, a set of keys fell through the hole in the glass.

"Thank you." Mox said, grabbing the keys. "C'mon Priscilla."

"No traffic! And no smoking!" the attendant yelled as they walked out.

Mox went to get their belongings from the car, while Priscilla took Brandi to the room. As soon as they made it to the room, Brandi rushed into the bathroom to handle her business. Mox returned to the room a minute later and took a seat in the chair next to the window, while Priscilla sat on the bed. "Please tell me you didn't leave those Ki's in that house."

Priscilla sighed and shook her head. "What do you think, Mox? You rushed me. I left everything. What part of that don't you understand?"

Mox stood up from the chair and paced the floor. "How the fuck you leave ten kilos in that house, Priscilla?"

"First of all... lower your voice and stop fuckin' cursing at me!" Priscilla shouted.

Mox sat back in the chair and squeezed his temples. It couldn't get any worse than this. They were on the run, broke, and the work they thought they had was gone. Out of nowhere, a sharp pain stung the entire right side of Mox's body. He grabbed the back of his head and bent down between his legs in excruciating pain. Priscilla didn't realize what was going in until he collapsed to the floor, holding his head.

"Mox... what's wrong? Mox! Mox!" She screamed, rushing to his side, trying to lift him off the floor.

"I'm good... I'm good..." He said, holding onto the bed to stand up. "What the fuck jus' happened?" he asked.

The toilet flushed and they both looked towards the bathroom as Brandi walked out.

"Brandi, you alright?" Priscilla asked.

"Yes," she answered.

Mox fixed himself and went into the bathroom to splash some water on his face. As he gazed into the cloudy mirror, his thoughts went back to the shooting.

Cleo had the pistol clutched tightly in his hand. It was pointed directly at Mox's head. He cringed when the shot went off, and it seemed as if it were happening all over again. The sharp pain resurfaced and Mox almost fell into the tub. Luckily, he caught hold of the shower curtain and somehow got back to his feet.

What the fuck is wrong with me? He kept asking himself.

And then he remembered. Before he was released from the hospital, the doctors told him he would suffer sporadic pains throughout his body, but he never thought they would feel the way they did. He ran the cold water from the faucet, splashed a handful on his face, and dried off with a towel that was on the rack. By the time he stepped out from the bathroom, Brandi was knocked out, laid across the bed.

"Damn... she was tired," he said. "How you feelin'?"

Priscilla didn't answer, she just rolled her eyes. "You still mad, Priscilla?" Mox walked to the end of the bed where Priscilla sat. "I know you hear me talkin' to you." He bent down and gazed into her eyes. "Gimme a kiss."

"Move Mox. Don't touch me." Priscilla pushed him out of her face.

"I can't have a kiss?"

"No. Go kiss your other bitch."

Mox looked over at Brandi to make sure she was asleep. "My other bitch, what are you talkin' about, Priscilla?"

"Mox, don't fuckin' play stupid wit' me... you know the bitch I'm talkin' about."

"Priscilla..." Mox went to grab her arm, and she stood up and slapped the left side of his face.

"I said don't fuckin' touch me!" she yelled.

A silent stillness settled in. Mox grabbed his cheek and shook his head. It took everything he had in him not to react, but one slight glance at his sleeping beauty on the bed and his mind was made up. "I'm goin' out." He said, snatching the car keys off the table.

Priscilla didn't ask where he was going, she just listened as he walked out and slammed the door. Her hands began to shake, and tears welled up in her eyes as she sat at the edge of the bed, jumbled and lost in her thoughts. *Was this a test of their loyalty? How strong was their love?* She asked herself a thousand questions, and finally concluded that Mox was the only man she ever loved and the only man she wanted to be with—the man she wanted to spend the rest of her life with.

CHAPTER THREE

Mox slowed to a stop when the traffic light turned red at Watson & Leland Avenue. He glanced down at the gas gauge and noticed it was almost on empty. He thought about how much money he had in his pocket. "Fuck!" he banged the steering wheel with a closed fist. When he looked up, the light was changing to green. He pressed the gas pedal and cruised by two bystanders that were on the corner. As he slowly passed, he recognized one of the men and pulled to the curb. "Yo, Bing!" he called out.

"Who the fuck is that?" one of the men mumbled. He was wearing a grey hooded sweatshirt, jeans and ACG boots. He tapped his partner, took a step back, and reached into the front pocket of his sweatshirt.

"Who you?" the other man asked.

Mox cut the car off and started to get out.

"That's Mox?"

"Yeah nigga... wassup?"

The chubby Spanish kid with braids looked back at his partner and gestured for him to put his weapon away. "Everything good," he said, approaching Mox. "How you, what the fuck happened?" He was staring at the patch on Mox's eye.

"Shit got real. Nigga shot me in my face... tried to dead me."

"Yeah, I see... goddamn." They shook hands and Botta Bing introduced his homeboy. "Yo, Mox, this my nigga, Luck. Luck, this Mox. We was in the joint together for a minute... so what's good, fuck you doin' over here?"

Mox looked around. The streets were barely alive and the only movement was a passing taxicab every few minutes. "You busy? Come take a ride wit' me."

Botta Bing peered up the block. "Shit kinda slow out here anyway." He walked around to the passenger side and opened the door. "Yo Luck, hold this shit down. I'll be right back." Mox pulled away from the curb and kept straight on Watson Avenue. The quiet Audi engine purred and the music played at a moderate level.

"So, what's good?" Bing asked. He saw the annoyance on Mox's face as he handled the steering wheel. "I see you got somethin' on your mind, huh?"

Mox shook his head and kept one hand on the steering wheel. "Honestly, I got a bunch a' shit on my mind. Kinda fucked up, Bing... I need a come up."

Botta Bing watched as the traffic passed. "A come up like what?"

"A few hunit thousand... sumptin' light."

"Shiiid... the only way you gettin' that is if you take it."

"Show me where it's at."

"You serious, huh?"

Mox looked over to Botta Bing and then pulled the car to the curb and parked. "Look at me, my nigga," he said. "This is it. This all I got. If I gotta go upside a nigga head to get mines... then so be it. But one thing for sure... ain't no way I can live like this."

Bing sensed the urgency in Mox's voice and paid close attention to his body language. He could tell if a person was being honest or not, just by the way they maneuvered. He knew Mox's words were truthful and he was willing to help him out. "So what you workin' wit'?"

Mox turned and stared. "I told you..." he ran his hand over the steering wheel. "This is it. This everything I got right here."

Botta Bing pulled his cell phone from his pocket and dialed a number. After a brief conversation, he told Mox to pull off and directed him to their next destination. Fifteen minutes later, he pointed to a garage they were coming up on and told Mox to pull into it.

Mox eased off the gas and made the right turn into the cluttered garage. He turned the lights off and snatched the key out of the ignition. "Fuck is this shit?" he asked, looking around the dark, dampened space.

"Chop shop nigga... gon' see what my man can give you for this joint." Bing said.

Mox looked around Priscilla's car. He knew she would have a fit once she found out he got rid of it. It was only thing she had—it was the only thing *they* had.

"How much you think I can get for it?"

"I don't know," Botta Bing knocked on the hidden steel door at the rear of the garage. It was covered with a *Wu Tang Clan* poster. "We 'bout to see though." he said, as they waited.

Less than a minute passed and someone on the other side of the door answered. "Who dat?" his voice was deep and he had a heavy Jamaican accent.

"Bing!" Seconds later the door came open and Mox followed behind Botta Bing as they entered the hidden area. It was a dimly lit space that had a cool breeze flowing through. Mox noticed the several parked cars to the far left and the faint aroma of marijuana.

"Wha gwaan bredren?" A tall, slinky Jamaican with a shiny bald head, crooked teeth, and a matching suit greeted.

"Every ting cool," Bing answered. He switched his accent to mimic the Jamaican. "Mi have a nice toy fa ya' Ras."

The Jamaican scratched his chin and sucked his teeth. "Um hmm..." he pointed to the door and the three of them walked out. "Two tousand eleven Audi..." He said, opening the front door. He sat down in the passenger seat. "She ot?"

"Huh?" Mox didn't understand him.

"I said, is she ot?"

Mox looked over to Botta Bing.

"Nah... she good Ras," Bing replied. "It's paid for right, Mox?"

"Oh... yeah, yeah... paid in full. Everything's legit." Mox assured.

The Jamaican continued to inspect the car. He popped the trunk and walked around to the back of the vehicle where Mox and Bing were standing. "Mi give ya' twelve tousand cash."

"*Twelve stacks?* Nigga, we look like crackheads to you?" Bing was insulted.

Ras sucked his teeth even harder. "Mi nah call ya' crackhead bredren."

"We need twenty-five." Bing said.

"Blooood claaaatt... mi nah give ya' twenty-five bredren. Twenty-five too high."

"Twenty-five or nothin'" Bing's negotiating skills were superb. *Always go with the high number* was his motto. He looked Ras dead in his eyes without blinking.

"Eighteen bredren..."

"Fuck outta here." Bing tapped Mox on his shoulder and turned to leave. "C'mon son, we blowin' this joint, I'ma take you to my man in Queens... he gon' treat you right." He said. His voice was low, but loud enough for Ras to hear him.

"Hol' on, hol' on..." Ras sucked his teeth once more and cut his eye at Mox. "Twenty-two?" he said.

Bing looked at Mox and Mox slightly nodded.

"Twenty-two might do." Botta Bing said. He really wanted to crack a cheese smile from ear to ear, because he knew Mox was going to look out for him after this deal. "How long before you gon' have it?" he asked.

"Mi have it now bredren, tree minutes ya' gimme." Ras said. He walked back into the garage area and returned in less time than he predicted. When he came back, he was holding a small black bag that he tossed to Mox. "Count it."

After Mox counted the money, they left out and Botta Bing flagged down a taxi cab. "Take us to Harlem." He announced to the driver who had tan skin, short black hair and a pointy nose. "And roll the windows down. I can smell ya' hot ass breath all the way back here."

"What's in Harlem at one o clock in the mornin'?" Mox inquired as he slid into the backseat of the Town Car.

"We gon' go see my man Snap. He got some shit. This the city that never sleeps kid, get used to it." Bing tapped the back of the driver's seat. "Yo, I asked you to roll the windows down man. It fuckin' stink back here." the driver ignored him and kept his eyes on the road, so Bing tapped the back of his seat a little harder the second time. "Yo, Habibi roll-the-fucking-windows-down, please?"

The driver finally looked into the rearview mirror. "My name is not Habibi." he said.

"I don't care what the fuck ya' name is... jus' roll the windows down."

For the first time, the driver turned in his seat to see the face of the man who was cursing at him. His eyes met Botta Bing's and then he looked at Mox—the windows slowly came down. He was aware of the recent area shootings and figured he keep his mouth shut tonight, even though he hadn't had the best day himself.

"Fuckin' Arabs..." Bing mumbled. He relaxed in his seat and stared out the window. It took them approximately 22 minutes to reach 131st street and Adam Clayton Powell Jr. Blvd. in Harlem.

Mox passed Bing a twenty-dollar bill. He paid the driver and they stepped out of the vehicle.

Mox surveyed his surroundings as soon as the door shut, and the cab pulled off. Harlem was unfamiliar territory. He barely knew Botta Bing, but here he was, standing in the middle of the street with over twenty thousand cash in his pocket and not a weapon within arm's reach to defend himself if need be. But he moved on instinct and went with his gut feeling. As far as he was concerned, Botta Bing was a stand up dude. He looked out for Mox when he really didn't have to, so on the strength of that alone, Mox had respect. Although the streets were a different playground, he knew how to play his cards and Mox knew not to overstep his boundaries.

They crossed the street and headed into the Saint Nicholas Housing Projects, but Mox stopped short. "You got me in a nigga projects at one in the mornin'? I ain't feelin' this, my nigga," he said, watching a car cruise down the block.

Botta Bing let out a sigh and shook his head. "My nigga..." he reached in the waistline of his pants, pulled out a black handgun and cocked it, placing a round in the chamber. "Ain't nothin' gon' happen to you. I got you, my nigga... that's my word." He cautiously looked around and then stuffed the gun back into his pants.

Seeing the gun eased Mox's nerves. He felt better about the situation, so they continued their walk into the building. Upon entering, a few muffled voices could be heard in the staircase around the corner and the sour, potent smell of marijuana lingered in the air. Bing and Mox kept their eyes and ears open, but didn't pay too much attention to the chatter a few hundred feet away. They took the elevator up four flights and approached apartment 4D.

Botta Bing knocked on the door. "When we get in here, jus' let me do all the talkin'." he said.

They heard footsteps coming towards the door and then the lock clicked. "Come in, Bing." Someone behind the door said. "Lock it behind you."

Bing and Mox entered the apartment. It was hot and it smelled like someone was cooking something. The short hallway leading to the living room area was pitch-black and Mox could barely see in front of himself; he almost bumped into Botta Bing. As they walked further into the living room, a shaded lamp that sat atop an end table in the left corner provided minimal light—just enough to see the person's face you were talking to.

Snap pulled a cigarette from his pack, lit it and took a seat in his favorite lounge chair. "So, what's good, Bing. What can I do for you today?" he asked, taking a hard drag off the cigarette. He was short, dark skinned, overweight, and trying to hold on to what little bit of hair he had left on his head. But deep in his heart, he knew he needed to cut it.

"I need a few pieces." Bing said, pushing some clothes on the couch aside so he could sit down.

Snap turned to Mox and exhaled the smoke through his nostrils. "You ain't gon' introduce your friend?"

Bing stood back up. "Oh, yeah... my fault. But the last time I bought somebody through you told me you didn't wanna meet 'em."

"This ain't last time," Snap replied. "And this guy looks interesting."

"That's my boy, Mox." Bing said.

"*Mox?*" Snap took another long pull of the cigarette and blew the smoke in Mox's direction. "What happened to your eye?"

"I got shot." Mox answered.

"Damn... you gotta be a strong muthafucka to get shot in head and live to tell about it. I guess God was on your side huh?" Snap plucked the ashes in a plastic cup that was sitting on the coffee table in front of him. "You a cop?"

"C'mon Snap, you kno—"

"Shut up Bing." Snap sat up in his seat. "I'm talkin' to Mox right now. I asked you if you was a cop?" he questioned again.

"Nah, I ain't no cop." Mox could see he was easing his right hand down into the cushion of his chair, more than likely reaching for a gun. He must have blinked his eye, because before he could even think about what to do, a pistol was pointed at his head.

"Oh. Alright..." Snap clutched the black and chrome weapon with the confidence of a sharp shooter. "Because I don't mind shootin' a couple of dem muthafuckas." he let the clip drop from the bottom of the gun, caught it, pulled the barrel back and then dumped the bullet that was in the chamber onto the carpet. He smiled at Mox and tossed the gun to Botta Bing.

"How much?" Bing asked, looking over the shiny, brand new weapon.

"A stack."

"How many you got?"

"How many you need?" Snap asked.

Botta Bing looked at Mox and saw him flash two fingers. "Two." He said. "And lemme get like ten boxes of bullets."

"That's it?"

Bing looked to Mox again for an answer. "Nah... I need somethin' big too... street sweeper type shit." Snap thought on it for a moment, and then told Bing and Mox he'd be right back. When he returned, he was holding a large green duffle bag and wearing his signature sinister grin.

"Sumptin like this?" he asked, pulling a black machine gun from the bag and aiming it at the far wall. "What you think?"

"Yeah..." Bing smiled at the sight of the weapon; violence excited him. "I think that'll do for now." He glanced to his right, and Mox was giving him the head nod. "Yeah, we good wit' that."

After they got the money situated, Snap found his cleaning kit and touched the artillery up before they left. Due to his time spent in the military, he became a divine weapons specialist and could basically tell someone any and everything they needed to know about a gun. He was highly skilled in that area. His ability to dismantle and reassemble a weapon in less than 60 seconds was phenomenal and always a surprise.

Mox watched as Snap's hands moved quickly and quietly. He hadn't smiled or said a word—it was total concentration. He had all three guns cleaned and ready for use in less than 15 minutes. Once he finished, he pulled another cigarette from his pack and lit it.

"All ready to go." he said, blowing smoke through his nostrils. "Make sure that money right, and slam the door on the way out. I gotta take a shit; I'ma see you later."

Snap disappeared into the back while Mox and Botta Bing gathered the weapons and quietly left the apartment. They opted for the steps instead of the elevator. Dodging the urine puddles and piles of trash that littered the staircase, they finally made to the lobby and out the building. Botta Bing waved a cab down in not time. "Yo, come see me in the AM. I'ma take you to my other peoples and get you some wheels for the time bein'." He said, seeing the cab pull up.

Mox gave him a pound, reached in his pocket and handed Bing a stack of twenty-dollar bills. "Good lookin' Bing..." Mox said, as he got into the backseat of the cab. "A nigga ain't got too many people he can rely on. I appreciate that shit."

"No doubt, my nigga, be safe." Bing closed the door and the cab pulled off. As soon as it was out of sight, he pulled his cell phone out, dialed a number and walked down the block.

CHAPTER FOUR

When she heard the key jiggling in the door, Priscilla sat up, pressed power on the remote, and

fixed her hair as if she wasn't just in dreamland. She glanced down to her left, to make sure Brandi was still sleeping, and indeed, she was—curled up, with her feet hanging off the bed.

Mox slowly and quietly entered the room, thinking Priscilla and Brandi would be sleeping at this hour. He didn't want to disturb their rest, knowing their situation, but as the door opened wider, he could hear the television. "You still up?" he asked, seeing Priscilla sitting up in the bed.

"Why are you comin' in here at four o clock in the morning, Mox?"

"I had to take care of somethin', Priscilla."

"You had to—" she stopped herself in mid-sentence and got up from the bed. "You know what... gimme my keys. We been in here all night, Mox. Your daughter and I are hungry. That didn't cross your mind?" she reached for her pants that were folded on the chair.

"I had to get rid of the car."

Priscilla let her pants fall to the floor and she plopped down on the bed. "What are you talkin' about, Mox?"

"I had to sell the car so we could get some money." He said, pulling the wad of cash from his pocket.

"I know you didn't sell my fuckin' car, Mox." Priscilla was in disbelief.

Their voices caused Brandi to squirm in the bed and roll over onto her stomach, so Mox pointed to the bathroom and Priscilla followed him.

As soon as the door closed, she went off. "You sold my fuckin' car! What the fuck is wrong wit' you, Mox? Did that fuckin' bullet fuck you up that bad?"

Mox grabbed her shoulders, pinned her against the wall and got right in her face. "Keep ya' fuckin' voice down before you wake my daughter up." He stared in her eyes. They were getting watery "What we got Priscilla, huh?" Before she could say anything, he answered. "Nothin'! Not a fuckin' thing! And you worried about that car... you can't be serious. I don't think you get it... we on the run. this shit ain't no game. We needed money, so yeah, I sold the fuckin' car."

Priscilla took a deep breath and shook her head. "I can't live like this, Mox. I can't do it."

"You don't have a choice, Priscilla. What you gon' do, turn yourself in? 'Cause I know you don't think I am, and Brandi is stayin' wit' me."

"*Wit' you?* And what are you gonna do, Mox, live on the street... goin' from hotel to hotel? That ain't the life for a little girl, and you know it."

"That ain't the life for nobody, Priscilla, but right now it's our life." Mox leaned against the wall. He couldn't even look in her eyes; it hurt too much. "I don't wanna lose y'all, I swear I don't, but I ain't never goin' back to that hell."

Priscilla's cries grew heavier and the tears dripped faster. "I don't know what to do, Mox. I don't..."

"Let me take care of us Priscilla, on everything I love... ain't nothin' gon' happen to either one of you." He snatched the bankroll from his pocket again. "Look, I got twenty thousand here. In a few hours, I'ma get us another car and we'll be good. We should have enough for a half a brick after that. We can take that and start over. Fuck everything else."

Priscilla fell into his arms and let her tears flow. She let all of her worries out on his chest. Hoping and praying that every word he spoke would be true. Although she knew that going back to the lifestyle would jeopardize everything—*what else was there to do, where else was there to turn?*

Mox held her soft warm body in his arms. She felt good in his clutches. It was the best feeling in the world—a feeling of fulfillment, pleasure and solace. He squeezed tighter; inhaling her sweet, lustful scent—it made him smile inside. He held on for dear life, never wanting to depart. He stepped back and looked at her puffy, red eyes. Mox wanted to cry. It pained his heart to witness the love of his life go through so much sorrow. The discomfort she felt— he also felt it, and whatever he could do to change it, he would do. He lifted her chin, moved in closer, and their lips met.

"Mox, I—"

"Shhh..." Mox put his finger to her lips. "I got you.," he whispered, stepping over to the shower. He turned the water on and made sure it wasn't too hot and then he started to undress her.

Priscilla wiped her tears and got into the hot shower. The warm beads of water immediately alleviated some of her built up strain as she stood under the showerhead. She looked at Mox and a half a smirk appeared on her face as she reached her hand out to him.

"Come on..." she whispered.

Mox stripped off his clothes and stepped into the shower behind her. He grabbed a washcloth from the rack, and some soap, and began washing Priscilla's back. He washed her entire body from head to toe, and then she did the same to him.

He whispered in her ear. "Do you trust me, Priscilla?"

She didn't verbally respond. She wrapped her arms around his waist and pulled him close. "Fuck me." She said, shoving her hot tongue in his mouth.

He reached down, palmed the cuff of her ass cheeks and squeezed until his dick hardened, and then he slid his middle finger into her steaming vagina from the back. Halfway in, he felt the wetness build up, and Priscilla let out a short sigh of pleasure. Mox spun her around, put her back against the wall—while the soothing hot water rained on their bodies—and Priscilla slightly raised her leg to let him slide in the middle.

She reached down, squeezed his ass cheeks and forced Mox to thrust himself into her. The temporary pain was her pleasure. It was something she desired—something she longed for. Her eyes rolled to the back of her head and she tightened the walls of her vagina around Mox's stiff erection. "Fuck me, Mox. This is your pussy baby..." She brushed the tip of her tongue across his bottom lip, and Mox dug deeper. He pushed himself so far into her kitty, it felt like he was touching her back.

"I love you, Priscilla," he whispered.

Their fuck session lasted twenty minutes before they both reached a climax and drifted into heaven. The entire time they thought Brandi had been sleeping, but in fact, she was up. She had her ear pressed against the bathroom door, trying to figure out what her parents were doing. All she could hear was running water and faint moans. She had an idea of what was going on, and cracked a smile before jumping back into the bed.

After a few hours rest, Mox was back up and ready to tackle the day's agenda. He knew for sure that they couldn't stay in one place too long, so while he slept; he plotted their next move.

"Priscilla, wake up." He said, tugging at the covers. "I'ma make this run, and I'll be right back. I left some money for you and Brandi to eat." He pecked her forehead and headed for the door.

"Mox," Priscilla called. He turned around before stepping out. She smiled and whispered. "I love you..."

"I love you too, babe, see you in a minute."

———————

Mox jumped out the taxi at the same spot he met Botta Bing the previous night, but the block was empty. He walked a couple hundred yards down the strip and took a peek in the corner store, but no one was there either, so he waited. He waited almost two whole hours before he saw Bing come bopping up the block.

"Damn nigga, I been out here all mornin' waitin' for you. It's cold as fuck, too."

"I know my nigga, my bad." Bing apologized, passing him a brown bag.

"What's this?"

"I got the call you was out here... so I know you ain't eat. I stopped by the breakfast spot before I came, had to fill up the tank." Bing rubbed his belly and giggled. "You ready?"

"Yup."

"Aight, let's do it."

He flagged a cab down and told the driver to take them to Brooklyn.

Mox purchased a Black 2004 Buick Regal with smoke grey leather interior for five grand. He slapped a dealer's plate in the rear windshield and he and Bing did 90 mph all the way back uptown, to the Bronx.

"Yo, Bing good lookin'." Mox said, sitting in the driver's seat.

"No problem, Mox," Bing gave him a pound, pushed the passenger side door open and got out. "Be safe out here... don't let them suckas get one up on you. If you need me, you know where to find me."

Mox nodded and then pulled off, merging with the already flowing traffic on the busy Bronx Borough Street. Before he returned to the room, he did a little shopping. Besides the underclothes and toiletries he bought, he also snatched up two Boost

Mobile phones and a few extra sim cards. He was conscious of the consequences and aware that life on the run wasn't sweet, and one slip up could cost them their freedom, so Mox followed his plan to the tee; never leaving anything out.

He needed to replenish old relationships and make them new again. It was imperative that he get back on his feet, and he knew just the person to contact. As soon as he found another spot for Priscilla and Brandi to stay in, he would go through the necessary channels to get the phone number he needed.

———

Brandi rushed to the door when she heard a key enter the lock. "Daddy!" she shouted, attaching herself to Mox's leg as he stepped through the door. "Mommy brought McDonalds."

"Oh yeah, where is it?"

Brandi threw on her sad puppy face. "We ate it all." she said.

"You *ate* it all? And you didn't save Daddy any? That ain't right."

Brandi laughed when Mox put his sad face on and acted like he was crying. "Don't cry Daddy, McDonalds is right across the street." She giggled. "You can go get some more."

Mox dropped the bags he was carrying, reached down and scooped Brandi in his arms. He kissed her forehead and her cheek. "You know Daddy loves you, right?"

"Yes."

"You love Daddy?" he asked.

"Yes."

"Does Mommy love Daddy?"

Brandi looked at Priscilla and then back to Mox. "Yeeesssss!" she sang, in the most innocent, child-like voice.

Mox put on a smirk and looked at Priscilla. "Let's get outta here."

CHAPTER FIVE

Oak Grove, South Carolina

"Yo, that don't look like a zone, mane."

"It's all there. I wouldn't short you, homey." Cleo assured. "I don't do business like that."

The kid standing in front of Cleo was tall and skinny. He had cornrow braids, a white t-shirt, blue jeans, and a pair of dusty Jordans on. He held up the plastic baggie with the large white rock of cocaine in it. He examined it a few more seconds and then tossed it back on the table in front of Cleo.

"Nah... I don't want that shit, mane. Lemme get my bread back."

"Get your *bread* back?" Cleo stood up from behind the table. "Nah, I don't work like that. Get the fuck out my gate."

"C'mon mane... it's like that?

"Yeah, it's like that." The kid reached down to grab the plastic baggie off the table and Cleo pulled his gun out. "I said get the fuck outta here... now."

The only thing he could do was put his head down and walk out the trailer. He knew Cleo would kill him if he made another move, and that little bit of work wasn't worth getting killed over. He realized he should have taken it when it was given to him. Now he was leaving out with nothing, and on top of that, he felt humiliated.

Cleo tossed the gun on the table next to the bag of cocaine and lit his blunt. "Yo, Whoadie, lock that door." he said.

Whoadie was Cleo's right hand man since his relocation to the south. They met through a female who was a mutual friend to both of their respective women. Immediately, they took a liking to each other and formed a bond. Whoadie was just the type of person Cleo was looking for; somebody of his caliber—someone just as grimy, self-centered and disloyal as himself. Someone he could expunge easily, with no regrets.

"If you see that nigga come back down that road, you know what to do." Cleo said.

"Umm hmm..." Whoadie nodded. He was 5 ft. tall, 150 pounds, brown skinned with nappy box braids in his hair. His pants were always sagging past his butt, and it was like his white t-shirts came with stains on them, but his gun worked like new, and he was itching to put it to use.

Cleo hit the blunt and passed it. "I went through a whole thing last night." He said, counting a stack of money. Since his departure from New York, Cleo had settled in the small country town of Oak Grove, South Carolina. He fit in perfectly. It wasn't much going on, and that's just the way he wanted it to be. He was renting a trailer home tucked away in the cut on Wren Road, and after a robbery he and Whoadie pulled off, Cleo was supplying the town with cocaine. He was making $20,000-$30,000 a day, and he didn't have a worry in the world. The last thing he was thinking about was Mox and all the bullshit he left back home. "Yo, Whoadie... roll up another joint and come help me count this money."

April 2012 - New York, New York

Gloomy, grey clouds hovered over the city's skyline, causing a cool breeze to drift off the Hudson River. It had been raining only 20 minutes ago, and it looked like the sun wanted to break through the clouds; only it couldn't. Mulberry Street wasn't crowded, but it also wasn't empty. A handful of pedestrians milled about the restaurants and retail shops as they did daily.

Inside Pelligrino's restaurant, Vinny Telesco sat relaxed in his seat, at his usual table in the rear of the establishment. An empty plate and half a drink was in front of him and a handkerchief was tucked in the front of his shirt.

"Aye, Mikey... what time is it?" he asked his son.

"Two o'clock, Pop, you got somewhere to go?"

"No, Mikey, I jus' wanna know the damn time. Is it too much?"

"Not at all pop... not at all..." Mikey went back to reading the day's paper when the sound of the jingling bells on the entrance door made him turn around.

A teenage kid with the same name as Vinny's oldest son came rushing through the door. "Vinny! Vinny! Mikey!" he shouted, running to the back.

Mikey hopped up from his seat and stopped the kid once he passed the bar. "Hey, hey, hey... hold up kiddo. What's the rush about?" he questioned.

Young Mikey was out of breath. "There... there... there's a dead... dog out front."

"A dead dog?"

"Yeah, c'mon." young Mikey snatched older Mikey's hand and led him outside.

"What the fuck! Scooter!" Mikey yelled, rushing to the sidewalk. He kneeled beside the bloody German Shepard that was sprawled across the pavement. "Please... no... Scooter, wake up!" he picked the dog's head up and put his ear to his mouth to see if he was still breathing. "Please Scooter, wake up..."

Scooter was Mikey's pet dog that he had for more than 10 years. It was his best friend. When everyone else got on his nerves, Scooter always made him feel at ease. He was the true definition of 'Man's Best Friend' and now he was lying on the cold pavement with a steak knife in his ribs, and a note attached to it.

Mikey pulled the knife out his dog's chest and read the note:

You about to meet Scooter in heaven muthafucka!

Mikey smirked and shook his head at the piece of paper. As he was lifting his head, he heard the sounds of a motorcycle speeding up the block. By the time he looked up to see who it was, it was too late.

"Say hello to Scooter, muthafucka!" Tyrell was on the back of the motorcycle dressed in all black, aiming an assault rifle at Mikey. He squeezed the trigger, disbursing rounds through the air like miniature missiles, and anything in the way of those bullets met its fate. The few people that were on the street, scattered for their lives as they watched those beside them get gunned down.

"Be out! Be out!" Tyrell nudged Six, who was on the front of the motorcycle and they peeled off down Mulberry Street.

―――――――――

"Turn the channel, baby, I ain't tryna watch this bullshit all night." Uncle Earl took a puff of the *La Cubana* cigar he had between his fingers and blew the smoke to the ceiling.

"But I was watchin' this, Earl." Baby G replied.

"Bitch, turn the muthafuckin' channel fo' I slap the shit outta yo' stupid ass. That's your problem now... you don't fuckin' listen. When I tell you to do something... goddamn it, do it!"

"Alright, alright," She picked up the remote. "What channel you wanna watch, baby?"

"I don't know... put something informative on, the news or something." Earl puffed his cigar again, this time letting the sweet smoke filter through his nostrils as he relaxed in his Jacuzzi sized tub watching the 40-inch television on the wall. "Right there, right there…" he said, telling Baby G to stop at the channel 12 News. "Turn it up. I can't hear shit."

"…The incident happened this afternoon, right here in broad daylight on busy Mulberry Street." The reporter explained. "The gunmen were said to be riding on a motorcycle prior to pulling up in front of this restaurant and opening blind fire. In the midst of this horrifying incident, three people were killed, and two more were injured. Mikey Telesco, son of alleged reputed mob boss, along with 13 year old Michael Penella, and an unidentified middle aged woman were all gunned down not too far from where I stand."

"Shit!" Earl hopped out the tub and snatched his towel off the rack. "I know this muthafucka didn't jus' do this shit." He had a strong feeling on who the gunmen in the shooting were, and he knew retaliation would come sooner than later.

"What's wrong, baby?"

"Nothin', go get me some pants… and hurry up." Earl dried himself off and rushed into the master bedroom behind Baby G. He threw his pants on and tossed a shirt over his head. "Bitch, what the fuck is you sittin' there lookin' stupid for? Get the fuck up and go start the car!"

"You ain't tellin' me nothin' Earl... what's goin' on?"

Uncle Earl ignored Baby G and went to the closet. He snatched a small black box from the top, opened it and pulled out an envelope. The contents of the envelope contained the combination to his safe on the other side of town. He checked to make sure it was there, and then he stuffed the envelope in his pocket.

Before Baby G opened the door to go downstairs, someone knocked. She turned in shock and ran back towards the bedroom. "Baby," she whispered. "Baby... somebody's at the door," she pointed.

Earl dropped the book bag he was holding, unzipped it, and pulled out his chrome.38 Special. "Move," he pushed Baby G to the side. "Go wait in the room."

"But Earl..."

"Bitch..." through clenched teeth, he scolded her. "Go sit yo' ass in the goddamn room." He tucked the pistol in his waistline and covered it with his shirt as he approached the front door. "Who is it?" he asked.

"Priest." A voice on the other end answered.

"Who?" Earl wasn't sure he heard right.

"Priest!" the man shouted.

Earl shook his head. "Fuck..." he mumbled, and then checked his waist to make sure the pistol was secure. He undid the lock and opened the door. "Priest, what a surprise." he said, inviting him into his home.

"It shouldn't be a surprise," Priest replied, walking into the apartment. "You should be expecting this visit. It's long overdue."

"*Overdue?*" Earl shut the door and locked it.

"Yeah, overdue;" Priest looked around at the well decorated apartment. "I been locked up for a long time, Earl, I know you been eatin'... I see it."

"Wait, wait, wait... hol' up, let's keep our voices down, I got company." Earl led Priest into the living room and offered him a seat.

"Nah, I'll stand." He insisted.

"Well, at least have a drink wit' me." Earl offered. He walked to the mini bar and held up two glasses. "Yak, or champagne?"

"Neither," Priest was serious. "Listen Earl, I ain't come here to have a toast and sit on your couch and relax. You know why I'm here. Now stop bullshittin' before I get upset."

Earl sensed the tone in Priest's voice. He also saw the shift in his demeanor. "Okay, cool..." he said. "But I thought we discussed everything that needed to be talked about; and besides... I don't think this is the right time or the right place."

"Oh, it's the right time... and the right place." Priest was through playing games. "Where the fuck is my money, Earl?"

"Your money?"

"Yeah, *my* money," Priest said, as he reached for the gun in the small of his back. But Earl was quicker. He had his weapon drawn a few seconds before and when the shot went off, Baby G almost jumped out her skin.

The hot bullet hit Priest in the stomach and sent his 200 plus pound body crashing to the carpeted floor. His gun fell from his hands and Earl quickly kicked it from his reach.

Priest tried to sit up, but the pain was too much to bear. "You better kill me... muthafucka..." splatters of blood shot from his mouth.

"Looks like you gon' need to say that prayer for yourself this time." Earl held the gun with both hands as he steadied his aim on Priest's head. "Don't worry, you ain't gon' be needin' that money where you goin'..." He clenched his jaw and got ready to squeeze the trigger. "Tell my sister I said hi..."

Priest looked up and saw Baby G walking out of the room. "Your whole life is a lie, Earl..." He smiled, and a stream of blood mixed with saliva hung from his lip. "You should'a killed me when you had the chance... now you can tell her yourself, muthafucka." He rolled over on his side and the blast from Baby G's gun echoed throughout the moderate sized apartment.

Earl collapsed and fell through the glass coffee table, shattering it to pieces. Baby G somehow helped Priest get to his feet and they stumbled out of the apartment without being seen.

CHAPTER SIX

One Hour Later...

"Uncle Earl!" Mox called out, seeing the front door was cracked open. "Hold on, Priscilla. Wait here." He slowly pushed the door wide open and tip toed down the short hallway. "Uncle Earl!" he called again, but no one answered. The sounds of a television could be heard, but no voices.

When Mox stepped into the living room, his eyes immediately dropped to the floor where he saw his uncle stretched out, face down in a pile of shattered glass. A stream of blood was coming from the hole in his back where Baby G had shot him, but he was still breathing. "Priscilla, take Brandi downstairs!" Mox yelled, pulling his cellphone out. He dialed 911 and told the dispatcher an old white woman was being robbed, and at what address. Before they could ask Mox a question, he hung up.

Priscilla didn't need to see what was going on. She knew by the sound of Mox's voice there was a serious problem, and for him to tell her to go back downstairs meant he obviously didn't want them to see it. She snatched Brandi's hand and they took the stairs down to the lobby and out to the parking garage.

"Unc... wake up." Mox was taking a high risk staying back. He went even further by trying to turn his uncle onto his stomach so he could breathe. He understood if he touched anything, he would be a potential suspect, but he couldn't just turn his back on family; he hadn't been bred that way. "C'mon Unc..." he struggled to lift the dead weight. "Gotta get you up."

Mox managed to get uncle Earl into an upright position, which helped him take in more oxygen, but if the paramedics didn't arrive soon, he was going to die. The bullet struck his right shoulder blade and was lodged somewhere between his chest and back.

He was wheezing and his lips started to change color. "Mox... go..." he could barely get the words out, but Mox heard him.

"You know I don't wanna leave you here like this Unc, but I ain't got no choice." Mox peeked out the living room window to make sure police hadn't shown up yet. "Tell me who did this to you," he said. Earl stared at the wall in a daze. His eyelids were getting heavier by the seconds and his breathing was becoming erratic. He didn't answer. "Unc..." Mox bent down, put one hand on his uncle's shoulder and got right in his face. "Tell me who did this to you so I take care of it... c'mon Unc."

Earl was slipping into an unconscious state. His eyelids were fluttering and his mouth was twitching, but no words were coming from his lips. Mox heard the faint police sirens in the distance and got up to leave, but Earl grabbed his leg. He looked at his uncle—helpless, and on the verge of death, and when Earl looked into his nephew's eyes, a wave of guilt consumed his entire soul. The tears spilled down his cheeks as he tried to get the words out of his mouth.

"C'mon Unc... hold on baby... you gon' be aight. Breathe Unc... breathe..."

Earl finally caught enough breath to mumble what he expected to be his last words. "Your... fa...ther..." his voice was just above a whisper, but Mox heard it clearly.

"My father?"

Earl nodded yes. "Priest." He whispered again.

The room became silent for less than a few seconds. Mox listened closely. A dog was barking, birds chirped and a train was passing through the station. He listened for the sirens and they were getting closer with each second. His vision was getting blurry. He looked down at his hands and it looked like he had one hundred fingers. Mox felt woozy and suddenly a sharp pain shot through the right side of his body and weakened his knees. He reached for the arm of the couch, but his body weight was too much to hold up and he fell to the floor. The last thing he saw before closing his eyes was a silhouette of someone coming through the door.

The only light in the pitch-black sky was the full moon that looked close enough to touch. As the weed smoke funneled through his nostrils, Tyrell leaned against the trunk of his car. He thought about all he'd been thorough. The road he traveled had been a long, rough one, but he managed to weather the storm and come out on top. The only thing left to do was to buy his mother that big nice house he always promised her. And at the rate he was going, that house would be purchased sooner than later.

Furthest from his mind, was what had taken place only hours ago. A war with the Italians was in full swing. It was a battle he knew he couldn't win, but his pride wouldn't let him back down; especially after they murdered his cousin. What did bother him was the fact that he had also murdered a child—

an innocent child—a child who had no knowledge of what was going on.

Tyrell puffed the weed again and watched as a black Cadillac cruised down the block past him. It was unusually warm for a mid-April night, and everyone was taking advantage of the beautiful weather. Three nicely dressed young ladies crossed the street on their way to the corner store and walked pass Tyrell, giggling like they were talking about him. He knew all three of them.

"You jus' gon' walk by me like that Chrissy, I thought we was cool." he said.

"You full a' shit, Rell." Chrissy replied, turning around. "You were supposed to call me yesterday. What happened?"

"I got caught up. I didn't forget, though. I had some business I had to take care of."

"You didn't forget, but you also didn't call."

"I'm here now though... wassup?"

Chrissy's two friends were telling her to hurry up. "I gotta go. Maybe I'll see you later."

"Hol' up Chrissy..." Tyrell tried to get her to stop. "lemme me holla at you for a sec'."

"Chrissy, c'mon!" one of her friends shouted.

"They're waiting for me, Rell. I'll talk to you later."

Tyrell watched Chrissy's ass bounce as she walked away. "Fuck them bitches," he laughed. "They jus' mad ain't nobody tryna holla at them."

"Them bitches is broke anyway." Six added. He was sitting in the passenger seat of Tyrell's car with the door open.

"Yo, Six... hold me down. I'm 'bout to check mama love out real quick. I ain't seen her in a few weeks."

"Aight... I'll be right here."

Tyrell crossed the street and walked into the projects. The lights along the path to the building were all shot out, so he could barely make out the few people standing on the strip. A small radio played and the overwhelming stench of potent marijuana was prevalent in the air. He heard a few 'wassup's' and continued into his mother's building.

He knocked on the door once and then realized he still had his house key, so he checked his pockets, found it, and then opened the door.

The apartment was the usual mess. Dirty clothes and miscellaneous garbage was strewn throughout the entire living room. It was nowhere to sit. He had to move a pile of laundry just to see a seat on the couch. Tyrell looked around in disgust. He was ashamed and fed up with his mother's living conditions.

"Ma!" he called out as he maneuvered through the rummage.

"What Tyrell?" she answered.

"Where you at?"

"I'm in the bathroom goddamn it. What you want?"

"Pack your shit... I'm gettin' you outta here."

"Boy please..."she replied. The toilet flushed and she came out the bathroom. "And where am I goin' Tyrell?"

"Anywhere," he said. "I can get you an apartment uptown in that new building if you want."

"*Uptown?* Tyrell you gotta have money to live up there. I ain't got no goddamn money."

"Don't worry about the money, Ma. I'll take care of that... jus' pack up your stuff."

"I don't wanna go, Tyrell."

"Why not?" He couldn't understand why his mother wanted to stay in the projects.

"Because I said I don't want to." She picked up a half-smoked cigarette from the ashtray and lit it. "I don't know anybody over there, Tyrell. All those damn white people. I don't wanna be bothered wit' that."

"So, you rather live like this?" he said, looking around at the mess she was living in. "In the projects your whole life. I thought the main goal was to get out."

"Get out and go where, Tyrell? Ain't nowhere for us to go. You wanna go up there and live wit' all them damn white people, you go right ahead. I ain't goin' nowhere... now gimme some money."

Tyrell knew once his mother's mind was made up, there was no persuading her to change it. Nothing he could do or say would make her feel any different. Her words were stone—the final say so. He stared at her for a moment, trying to figure out why she felt the way she did, but he couldn't understand it—he didn't understand how you could struggle all your life, and then turn your cheek to an opportunity. It was something he would never understand.

He pulled a wad of cash out his pocket, peeled off $1,000 and gave it to her. "Let me know if you change your mind." he said, as he left out. "Make sure you pay some bills with that money too, and don't smoke it up."

Ms. Michaels's took a long drag of her cigarette and plucked the ashes on the floor. "Tyrell please... as far as I know, I'm the mother." she replied. "You don't tell me what to do, I tell you what to do."

Tyrell shook his head and closed the door. He went down the back staircase instead of the front because it was faster, but he had no idea someone was there waiting for him. As soon as he pushed the door open to go down the steps, Gahbe was right there waiting with his gun drawn.

"Surprise, nigga," he whispered, pushing the barrel of the revolver in Tyrell's face. "Told you I was gon' get that ass." Tyrell was caught off guard— slipping, but he kept his calm. If he could reach the gun at the small of his back, Gahbe would have a problem on his hands. "Run yo' shit nigga..." he demanded. With his free hand, he searched Tyrell's pockets. But when he went to touch his waistline, Tyrell moved. "Move again, nigga, and I'ma leave you right here." He promised.

Tyrell stayed silent. He knew Gahbe was scared; and he knew a scared nigga would shoot him in a heartbeat. He watched his hand shake while he held the gun. "You scared nigga..." He mumbled and tried to reach for the weapon, but Gahbe had a tight grip.

Tyrell pushed him into the hallway door and tried to take off down the steps, but Gahbe was on him. He leveled the pistol, aimed, and pulled the trigger. The echo from the blast was ear piercing. The slug tore a chunk of flesh from Tyrell's left leg, but he managed to make it out the building alive. He stumbled down the entrance steps and hobbled down the strip towards the block.

Gahbe realized he fucked up when Tyrell wasn't lying at the bottom of the steps, dead. He had to prepare himself for the repercussions, because they would come, and they would come sooner than later.

CHAPTER SEVEN

When Mox opened his eye, he was greeted by the most beautiful smile he had ever saw. The same smile he had fallen in love with years ago.

"Hey baby. How you feelin'?" Priscilla asked. She rubbed his head and then caressed the side of his face. He tried to sit up, but she made him stay in the bed. "Where you goin'?"

"Where are we?" he looked around and saw Brandi lying on the small leather loveseat at the other end of the room.

"The Harlem Flophouse," she answered. "Don't worry, we're good here."

Mox scanned the room. There was a large walnut dresser opposite the bed. The floors and door entrances were all made from real wood and the lighting was very dim.

"How we get here?" he asked. "I don't remember nothin'."

"You passed out, Mox."

"Passed out?"

"Yes..." she said. "Uncle Earl's house... you don't remember?"

"*Uncle Earl's house?*" Mox's memory was blank. He couldn't recall anything that happened. He let his head rest on the pillow, closed his eye, and took a deep breath. "Why was I was at my uncles house, and how the hell did I pass out?"

Priscilla hesitated. She didn't want to tell him what happened, but she had to. She couldn't even look him in the face when she said it. "Uncle Earl got shot, Mox."

"What you mean he got shot?" Mox sat up in the bed. "When did this happen?"

"It must've happened right before we got there. You told me to go back downstairs and wait for you, but you took too long, so I had to come and see what was goin' on. When I got back to the apartment I saw you and uncle Earl lying on the floor."

Mox rubbed his head. He was trying his hardest to remember something—anything. After a few minutes, pieces of what took place were slowly popping into his memory. Eventually he had enough pieces to put together at least what he thought had happened.

"I know who shot my uncle." He said.

"Who?"

"The same person who killed my mother..." he replied.

Priscilla dropped her head. She couldn't begin to understand the distress Mox had to deal with, knowing that the man who killed his mother and shot his uncle was still walking the streets. She knew his ego wouldn't allow him to let it go, and no matter what she said, there was no deterring him from finding this man and taking his life.

Mox got up from the bed and tried to get himself together.

"Where you goin'?" Priscilla questioned.

"We need more money. I need you to make that call."

"But Mox—"

"Let's not argue about this, Priscilla. Jus' make the call."

Ten minutes later, a meeting was set up for Mox to meet with the connect; Juan Carlos. But before that happened, he needed to make a visit to the Men's Warehouse to purchase a suit. In order for Juan to take him seriously, he needed to look the part. Mox learned early that money attracted money, and first impression was everything. Although he and Juan had known each other already, they hadn't personally done business, so this was something new. Mox bought a navy colored Joseph Abboud slim fitting suit for $700, and a pair of black imperial wing tipped shoes for $200. He was ready to go.

Two hours later, Mox was pulling up to the front entrance of the Malaga Restaurant located on 73rd street in Manhattan's Upper East Side area. The valet parked his car and he was greeted by a short Spanish guy with a bald head, thin mustache, and a clean suit.

"Mox?" he asked.

Mox nodded yes.

"Mr. Carlos is waiting for you.

The two men entered the restaurant. It was small, but well lit. Mox looked around at the pictures on the wall. The atmosphere reminded him of someone's home. It was comfortable. They walked past the granite-top seating areas and neared the rear of the restaurant where Juan Carlos sat at a table in the corner by himself. He stood and smiled when they approached.

"Mox." He said, extending his hand.

Mox shook his hand and replied. "Juan Carlos, pleasure to finally meet you."

"Yes, yes, it is. Wow..." He looked Mox up and down. "I remember the last time I saw you. You were sitting in the car when Priscilla came by to see me. You were a kid then, Mox. You're all grown up now." Juan Carlos embraced Mox. He hugged him tightly, patted him on his back and offered him a seat. "C'mon... sit down, let's talk."

Two red handkerchiefs, two plates and two champagne glasses adorned the table top, and a slim, average height Spanish woman with an apron on and her hair in a bun came from the back to take their order.

"How are you today, sir, would you like to start off with a drink?" she asked.

"Veronica, this is my good friend Mox. Mox, this is my niece, Veronica."

"Nice to meet you," Mox said, shaking the young woman's hand. "Yeah, I'll have some water please."

"Veronica, bring us two orders of patatas bravas please." Juan Carlos said. "So, what's up, Mox? Talk to me."

Mox relaxed in his chair. "It's like this Juan..." he explained. "I'm fucked up in the game right now. I got a lil' bit of paper to play with, but I need more."

"And you come here because?"

"Because I need your help."

"Haven't we been down this road before, Mox, what happened? What's gonna make this time different from the last?"

Mox took his time answering the question. He knew Juan Carlos wouldn't give him anything without proving himself first. "I grew up," he said. "I'm not the same young nigga without any direction. I know exactly what I want now."

"And what's that?"

He looked directly into Juan Carlos' eyes. "More money than I can think about counting." he replied. Mox knew how the game was played, because he played it; and he played it well.

Juan Carlos kept a straight face. He wasn't easily excited by anything. "I don't know about this, Mox. Every time I turn on my television, I see you and Priscilla. I'm taking a big risk dealing with you two." The waitress came back with two plates of food and placed them on the table. "Thank you, Veronica..." he waited until she left and continued. "Last time I spoke to Priscilla, she said it was over. What brought about this sudden change?"

"What else I'm gon' do? I got a baby girl to take care of and can't stand to see her not bein' able to get what she wants. I gotta provide that."

"Mox, you're a smart kid, always have been. I think you can do anything you put your mind to. It's up to you to want more. More for yourself—for your family."

"Exactly," he agreed. "And that's why I'm here today... because I want more, but I'm not a greedy person."

Juan Carlos giggled. "I see," he said. "You barely touched your food."

"This shit is spicy. What the hell is it?"

"Patatas bravas, it's cut up white potatoes in a spicy tomato sauce. Good right?"

Mox nodded yes, as he stuffed his mouth with the fiery potatoes. The two of them sat, ate and finished their plates of food and then Juan Carlos ordered a bottle of wine. Veronica brought it out and poured the men drinks.

"So, tell me Mox... what exactly is it that you want me to do?"

Mox wiped his mouth with the handkerchief and sipped his wine. "I need two," he said. "I got fourteen."

"Fourteen, huh," Juan Carlos rubbed his mustache and smirked. "Fourteen is only enough for a half of one, and you want *two?*"

"I know I'm a lil' short, but this is all I got, Juan. You know if I didn't need it I wouldn't be askin'."

Juan Carlos stared into Mox's eye and carefully studied his body language. He knew every word he spoke was sincere. "This is it, Mox," he replied, finishing the last bit of food on his plate. "This is the last time I do you or Priscilla a favor. I'm done."

"Thank you, Juan. I really appreciate this." Mox smiled.

"One question," Juan said. "How do plan on moving this work with all this other shit going on?"

"I got some people I used to deal with that moved south. I'm goin' to see 'em."

Juan Carlos snapped his fingers and the short Spanish guy with the bald head appeared out of nowhere. He spoke to him in Spanish and sent him off.

"Everything is good. Your product will be in the car when you're ready to leave. Now where's my money?"

Mox reached into his pocket, pulled out the wad of cash and slid it over to Juan Carlos.

"This is fourteen?"

"Everything I got."

Juan Carlos fingered the stack of money and then slid a few bills back to Mox. "Don't ever say I didn't look out for you," he said. They shook hands and Mox got up to leave.

CHAPTER EIGHT

Mox made a right turn into the parking lot and pulled into an empty space between a black Jetta and a grey Astro work van. He put the car in park and he, Priscilla and Brandi got out. The air was still. Not a breeze within miles, and the illuminated sun was shining bright. They walked through the front entrance of the hospital, and immediately, Mox felt a chill throughout his body. He despised hospitals and everything they stood for.

"You alright?" Priscilla asked. She could see the discomfort in his actions.

"Yeah, I'm good. How 'bout you?"

"I'm fine," she answered.

They continued down the corridor and approached the information desk. Two young black security guards sat in chairs behind a small wooden table. One of them—the younger looking of the two—was reading a magazine while the other guy watched sports on his iPhone. Neither one of them were paying attention, so the three of them slid right past. Mox pressed for elevator and they took it to the second floor.

"What's the room number, Priscilla?"

"Two ten," she answered, holding onto Brandi's hand. "I think this is it right here."

Mox turned the doorknob and slowly pushed the door open. He could see somebody lying in the bed. He knew it was his uncle, Earl.

"Wait here with Brandi for a second while I see what's goin' on."

Uncle Earl sat upright in his bed. His shoulder was wrapped in bandages, and he also had three Band-Aids on his face. His eyes were glued to the television and he held the remote in his hand, flicking through the channels. He hadn't acknowledged Mox enter the room.

"Hey, Unc, is that you?" Mox questioned.

Earl turned around with a half a smile on his face. "Hey wassup nephew, y'all come to get me huh?

Good, cause I wasn't about to spend another day in this muthafucka."

"Yeah Unc, we here for you." he lied. "Don't worry, I'ma get you up outta here." Mox had no clue they were letting his uncle go. It just so happened they showed up on the exact day of his release. "How you feelin'?"

Earl got up from the bed and started to gather his belongings. "I feel like shit, nephew. The food sucks, and every nurse that came through that door was horrible lookin'. They need to employ some pretty women up in here."

Mox laughed. "Yeah, I feel you, Unc."

Just as the two of them finished giggling, Jasmine walked in, followed by a not so happy looking Priscilla. She looked at Earl and then Mox, and she smiled. "Mr. Daniels, how are you today?"

"I'm fine nurse," Earl answered. "Damn you—"

"What the fuck is this bitch doin' here, Mox?" Priscilla cut in. She wasn't about to hold her tongue this time.

Mox was lost. He had no idea of what was going on, and was just as shocked as Priscilla. He hadn't thought about the possibility of bumping into Jasmine while visiting his uncle, but he did know that she worked there.

"C'mon Unc... let's get you outta here." He ignored Priscilla, but still felt the darts she was shooting at him from across the room. He knew her eyes were glued to him, so he didn't even turn around.

"Aww shit..." Earl sensed the tension and saw the fire in Priscilla's eyes. "Is that my baby girl right there?" he asked, diverting everyone's attention to Brandi.

"Mox, I asked you a question."

"Excuse me," Jasmine said. "I didn't mean to cause any problems. I'm just here to do my job."

Priscilla kissed her teeth and rolled her eyes as hard as she could. "Bitch, nobody was talkin' to you. Mind your business."

"Let's go, Priscila." Mox ordered.

"Oh... so now you don't wanna speak to your lil' friend, huh?"

"Stop it, alright."

"No Mox, you stop it. Ain't this the bitch you was fuckin' behind my back?"

Jasmine tried to avoid Priscilla's rant, but she wasn't about to be disrespected. "I'd appreciate it if you stop calling me out my name. I'm pretty sure you know what it is."

"Bitch, I'll—" Priscilla lunged at Jasmine, but Mox was right there to intervene. He grabbed her arm and pushed her into the hallway. He had her back pinned against the wall.

"Don't do this shit in front of my daughter. What the fuck is wrong wit' you?"

"What's wrong wit' *me?* You're the one who fucked that bitch!" she yelled.

"Lower your fuckin' voice."

"Fuck you, Mox. You better let that bitch know."

Jasmine had heard enough. "Alright, that's it." she dropped the clipboard she was holding and stepped towards the door where Priscilla and Mox stood.

"Ut oh… cat fight!" Earl shouted and grabbed Brandi's hand. "We better get outta here, Brandi. They trippin'."

Jasmine swung and almost hit Priscilla in her face, but Mox caught the blow because he was in the middle of them. Priscilla went to swing back.

"Priscilla, chill!" he warned, but she wasn't listening. She tried to escape Mox's hold and swing again, but she couldn't.

"Get off me, Mox!" She screamed. Tears of anger rolled down her cheeks. "Bitch, I'ma fuck you up!"

During the commotion, Uncle Earl had gathered his things, and he was ready to leave the hospital. "Y'all need to cut it out. Got this baby seeing all that nonsense. Control your women, nephew." He laughed.

"This shit ain't funny, Unc." Mox said. He was still holding Priscilla. He didn't want to let her go, because he knew she wouldn't stop once she got started. When he turned around, he saw the two security guards coming their way. "See, now this. Priscilla you know we can't afford to get caught up in this dumb shit. Let's go." He pulled her by the arm, but she jerked away and broke his hold. Before Mox knew what happened, Priscilla was on top of Jasmine like a lion pouncing on its prey.

One hand was full of Jasmine's hair, while she pounded her face with the other. The momentum caused them to fall to the floor and Priscilla landed on top. Mox tried to pull her up, but every time he pulled her, she pulled Jasmine. Priscilla was continuously banging the side of her face on the cold hospital floor. Blood shot from Jasmine's nose and mouth.

Uncle Earl also tried to intervene but his disabled shoulder and arm prevented him from doing so.

Brandi stood in the middle of the corridor, crying her young eyes out, begging her mother to stop. Priscilla looked up and saw the guards getting closer. They were on their walkie-talkies calling for back up, and she was pretty sure their back up was the police. She looked the other way and saw the hurt and embarrassment on her daughter's face.

Mox couldn't take it anymore. He grabbed Priscilla in a chokehold, pulled her off Jasmine and yelled for uncle Earl to get Brandi as they made a dash for the emergency exit.

"Damn son, that nigga got you good." Six teased as he stared at Tyrell's bandaged leg.

"Fuck you, Six. I'ma kill that muthafucka, and that's on everything I love. He can't walk these streets no more."

"That nigga outside right now. Want me to handle that?"

"Nah, this shit is personal. I wanna look that nigga in his eyes before I squeeze one in his dome."

"Here, hit this shit... take your mind off the pain." Six insisted.

Tiny pieces of sunlight crept through the small slits in the curtains as the two friends talked. Tyrell took the joint, hit it, and exhaled the smoke through his nose. He was sitting on a sofa with his leg propped up on an ottoman, and the only thoughts running through his mind were revenge. He was disgusted at himself for letting Gahbe catch him off point, but he wasn't taking it lightly. While he was laid up, he plotted.

"I got sumptin' nice for him... sumptin' real sweet for that bitchassnigga."

"What's that?" Six asked.

"Yo, Tia!" he yelled. "Hold on... watch this shit."

Tia came from the back room. She was tall, brown skinned and slim; like a runway model. Her hair was cut short, and she had thick full lips that longed to be kissed. She was one of the girls that Tyrell and Six used to transport their product from state to state. She was book smart, street smart, pretty, and she had her own car and apartment. She moved to New York a year ago so she could work in a strip club. Once Tyrell met her, he took her out the club and made sure she didn't want for anything. He set her up with an apartment in Pelham and kept her secluded from the street life. She was his favorite Mule.

"Yes, baby."

"Bring me that thang." Tyrell said.

Tia left the room and returned holding a long red box. She placed it on the floor in front of Tyrell and took the top off.

"Goddamn!" Six caught a glimpse of the heavy machinery that the box held. "Nigga, you plan on killin' everybody on the block, huh?"

"Hand me that, baby," Tyrell said to Tia. He held the assault rifle in his hands and looked up at Six. "They fucked up, Six... anybody out there when I come through is a target. Women, kids, innocent bystanders... I don't give a fuck. He violated, and I'ma deal wit' 'em the right way. I'ma show that faggot how to lay the murder game down, cause it's obvious he don't know what the fuck he doin'."

"No more kids, Rell. That shit was fucked up." Six tried his best not to think about what happened to the young boy the day they hit the Telescos, but the image of his small frame sprawled across the concrete in a pool of his own blood was imbedded in his mind. Since the day it happened, he hadn't had a good night's sleep, and he was sure he wouldn't get one anytime soon.

Tyrell grilled Six. He hated to be told what to do. "Them ain't cha muthafuckin' kids nigga, fuck is you worried about 'em for?"

"They kids, Tyrell, that's why. Shit, they could be mines, maybe yours... who knows. All I'm sayin' is... if there's kids out there, you need to rethink the situation."

Tyrell looked at Tia. "You hear this muthafucka? Who the fuck this nigga think he is, Tia?" Tia didn't answer; she just nodded in agreement. She didn't want to make the situation any worse than it already was. "Nigga, like I said... anybody out there is subject to get it. I don't give a fuck who it is." Tyrell placed the weapon back in the box and sent Tia to the back.

"We still makin' that move south?" Six asked. He wanted to change the subject.

"Yeah, after I murder this nigga... we out."

CHAPTER NINE

After Vinny Telesco buried his eldest son, he waged war and severed every tie he had to anybody that wasn't of Italian descent. Bodies started dropping up and down the eastern seaboard like flies, and everyone knew why, but nobody could stop it. He didn't know who pulled the trigger, but sooner than later stories started circulating. The first name to be mentioned was Mox Daniels.

Vinny relaxed in his leather lounge chair with his right leg crossed over his left. He held a burning La Gloria Cubana in one hand and a chrome and black Smith & Wesson.9 millimeter in the other. He knew he wasn't supposed to be smoking, but the added stress had him caring less about his health. He looked around the room. There were six guys; all hit men—all trained and ready to kill at the given word. The sweet stench of cigar smoke filled the air as he stared each man in the eyes.

"I'm gonna say this one time," he puffed the cigar, savored the flavor, and let the smoke escape from his mouth. "If you guys don't bring me that fucking nigger's head, I swear before God I'll kill each one you... now get the fuck outta my face."

None of the men said a word. They just left the room.

A few hours later, three of Vinny's men entered Frank's spot, Club Red and opened fire. Five people were shot and two were killed, one of them was Nate.

Priscilla's lips were poked out and she refused to step foot out the car. "I'm not going." she insisted.

"This is the only choice we got Priscilla, and you know as well as I do this visit is long overdue. Now c'mon." Mox insisted.

"I'm not leavin' my daughter with that lady. You must be outta your mind. I don't even know the last time I saw her. And now you want me to go up there and ask for help... you can't be serious, Mox."

Mox was becoming frustrated and the scorching sun wasn't helping at all. "I'm very serious, Priscilla. We can't have her seein' all this crazy shit. She's better off here wit' your mother."

Priscilla stared out the window at her mother's apartment building. She honestly couldn't believe she was even thinking about what Mox was saying, but the truth was that he was right. Their daughter had seen enough. The streets weren't the safest place to have your child out at all times of the night, and them being in the bind they were in caused Brandi to see more than her young eyes ever imagined.

Mox was fed up. He opened the passenger side door and grabbed Priscilla's arm. "Let's go..." he said, pulling her from the car. "C'mon Brandi, let's go see Nana."

Priscilla rolled her eyes as they walked to the entrance of her mother's apartment building. "She doesn't even know her, Mox. You can't force her to stay there."

"She's a child, Priscilla, she's gonna do what I tell her to do. And I think it's about time she get to know her."

"Get to know her, for what?"

"Because that's her grandmother, that's why. Don't you think it's a lil' selfish to not let her meet her grandmother? Just because you two had your differences doesn't mean Brandi has to suffer. She should know who her family is."

"She does know who her family is," Priscilla replied. "We're right here. We're the only family she needs."

As they were walking into the building, Mox stopped short. He stopped and thought about what Priscilla had just said. He thought hard about it. He held Brandi's hand, looked down at her precious, innocent little face, and then he looked up at Priscilla. "Well, what if somethin' happens to us, then what? What would she do then?"

The thought hadn't even crossed her mind. "Ain't nothin' happenin' to us, so we don't even need to discuss that," Priscilla said. She looked down into

Brandi's big beautiful eyes and wanted to cry. She couldn't fathom the thought of being separated again, and she would go to great lengths to make sure it didn't happened a second time.

She bent down and kissed her daughter's forehead. "You know Mommy loves you, right?" Brandi nodded yes. "And you know I would never let anything happen to you, right?" She nodded yes again. "Mommy needs for you to stay with your grandmother for a little while until things get situated. You okay with that?" Brandi half smiled and nodded yes once again.

They entered the building and took the elevator up. The ride was a silent one. Priscilla tried to encourage herself to be open minded and not dwell on the past, but it was difficult. It was a struggle for her to let go of the heartache caused throughout her childhood. She still felt a bitter taste in her mouth towards her mother. It was something that should have been addressed a long time ago, but wasn't.

Before the elevator door opened, Priscilla closed her eyes, took a deep breath and prayed that everything would be fine. She prayed that the slight amount of love she did have for her mother would override the hate and uneasiness she felt towards her. She prayed for her anger and emotions to remain intact, and she hoped she could stay calm and at least try to listen.

When the elevator stopped and the door opened, Priscilla watched Mox walk out while she stood in a daze. Brandi—more anxious than both of them—tugged at her hand as she stepped off the elevator.

"Mommy, c'mon... we're here." she exclaimed.

Priscilla snapped out of her trance and stepped off the elevator. All three of them stood in front of the door, but no one knocked. Priscilla looked over to Mox and he looked back at her. Brandi looked up at both of them and figured she'd do what they didn't.

"Who is it?" Ms. Davis asked hearing taps on her door.

Priscilla looked at Mox again.

"Mox," he answered. "I brought you a gift."

Ms. Davis undid the locks and slowly pulled the

door open. It was only cracked enough to see the face of the person knocking, because she hasn't heard the name clearly.

"Oh, that's you," she said, seeing Mox's face. "I wasn't expecting no company today. I thought you was one of those people selling something." As she spoke, she slowly opened the door all the way and when her eyes met Priscilla's, it was like everything around them came to a pause. They stared at each other for more than sixty seconds, just gazing— amazed, astonished and baffled, all at the same time.

"Y'all come on in and have a seat," she said. "Hurry up and close my door, you letting all the good heat out."

"It's nice out, Ms. Davis. What you doin' with the heat on?"

"I ain't as young as I used to be," she replied with a slight giggle. "Time catching up to me, baby. I ain't that spring chicken no more."

"Hi Grandma," Brandi mumbled as she stepped into the doorway.

"Oh my God," Ms. Davis covered her mouth with one hand and tossed the other on the air. "Is that my grand baby?"

Brandi's tight frown turned to a full-blown smile. "Yessss." she sang.

The corners of Priscilla's mouth went up. She couldn't hold the smile back if she wanted to. She watched Brandi embrace her grandmother. It was a first. It was the first time she had the chance to see how much love surrounded her. It was the first time she got to see her daughter interact with her mother—something that was long overdue.

Ms. Davis hugged her granddaughter for the first time, and realized how much she missed her. She hadn't seen her since she was born, and hadn't touched her until today.

"We're not stayin' long." Priscilla said, taking a seat on the sofa in the living room. She looked around at the pictures on the wall, and the ones on the mantle. Most of them were of her, and even though she had been taking care of her mother, she rarely visited and almost never called to check on her.

Mox snatched a picture off the top of the television, looked at it, and then handed it to Priscilla. "Remember this?"

"Of course," she said, marveling at the photo. "This was the day you got your car. I could never forget this day."

Ms. Davis sat in her favorite chair with Brandi in her lap, watching Priscilla and Mox. She could see the love radiate from their bodies. She knew it was a true love they shared, but they had a problem, and she also knew they needed her help. "So, what brings y'all by here to see me today?"

Mox placed the picture on the table. "We got a lil' problem, Ms. Davis," he turned to Priscilla. "Tell her," he said.

Priscilla hesitated.

"Tell me what?" Ms. Davis asked.

Priscilla stared at her mother's face. She was taken aback by how much she resembled her. She never wanted to look like her mother. She hated her mother.

"I know you seen the news because that's all you watch." she said. "I need you to take care of Brandi for a few days while we figure this thing out."

Ms. Davis heard her daughter talking, but acted as if she wasn't paying attention. Her focus was on Brandi.

Priscilla got annoyed. "See," she said, standing up from the sofa. "This is why I don't come here. She pays me no mind. Like I'm not even here."

Mox grabbed her arm. "Sit down and chill out."

"You know, I had a feeling you would come by here after I saw you on the news." Ms. Davis said. "Y'all done got all them people searching for y'all... you know that's dangerous, don't cha'. And you can't be running around here with this baby..."

"That's why we came to you, Ms. Davis. There's no one else we can trust to watch over Brandi."

Ms. Davis looked at her daughter. "Only if she apologizes."

"What!" Priscilla was livid. "Apologize, to you? You should be the one apologizing, not me!"

"Priscilla, calm down."

"No Mox... Mind your business."

"I'm not doing it unless you apologize."

"I can't believe you." Priscilla got up from the sofa again, this time she reached for Brandi, but her mother pulled her back. "Give me my daughter please, I'm leavin'."

Mox stood up and put his hand on her shoulder. "Hold on Priscilla, wait..."

"Get off me, Mox."

"Brandi's staying with me, but not under your circumstances, under mines." Ms. Davis picked her telephone up and dialed some numbers. "They're here." she said, and hung up. "See, I knew y'all would come here, so I called the police."

"You did what!" Mox ran over to the window and looked out. He didn't see any police.

Priscilla went to grab Brandi's hand, and Ms. Davis pulled a small knife from her brassiere. She wrapped one arm around Brandi's neck and held her close. "You make another move, and I'll cut her throat."

Mox was stunned. He couldn't believe what was

going on. "What the fuck is wrong wit' you?"

"Reward money, Mox. You think I'ma let that fifty thousand go to someone else when I can use it?" Ms. Davis was serious.

"Fifty thousand?" Priscilla was raging. "I told you we shouldn't have come here." She shook her head, reached into her purse, and pulled her gun out. "If you don't let my daughter go in two seconds, I'ma shoot you right in your fuckin' head."

"Priscilla, drop the gun... please, don't do this. Think about Brandi, think about our daughter Priscilla."

"Shut the fuck up, Mox!" She turned and pointed the weapon in his direction.

Ms. Davis snatched Brandi off her feet and pulled her into the bedroom a few feet way.

Mox backed away and put his hands in the air. "Priscilla... listen to me."

"No, Mox!" A river of tears poured from her eyes as she clutched the weapon in both hands. "I listened to you enough. That's the reason we're in this situation now."

A loud knock at the door made their heads turn. They looked at the door, and then at each other.

CHAPTER TEN

Pieces of pure white clouds were scattered throughout the crystal blue sky as a soft spring breeze rustled the leaves on the trees. School busses were pulling up to the entrance of the Hartley Housing Projects, and kids were jumping through the doors like they had been held captive for years. School was nearing its end, and the weather was getting warmer each day. Tenants sat on wood benches in front of their building gossiping about the previous night's endeavors—anxious to hear a story other than their own.

Tyrell leaned against the black gate in front of building 70. He had on a pair of black True Religion jeans, a white t-shirt, and some black and white Air Max 95's. It had been three weeks since he was shot, and he was healing much faster than expected. He held a cane in his right hand and a blunt in his left. "Yo, Six, send one of them lil' niggas to the store." he said.

Six was a few feet away, sitting on a crate, drinking a Pepsi and talking to his young boys.

"Yo, one of y'all niggas run to the store real quick." Six pulled some money from his pocket and gave it to the closest person to him. "Here..."

"Why I always gotta go to the store?"

"Yo Grasshopper, shut the fuck up and take yo' ass to the store before I slap the shit outta you."

Grasshopper looked at the seriousness on Six's face, sucked his teeth, and took a walk to the store.

Since the incident took place with Tyrell and Gahbe, the hood was on high alert. Everyone knew retaliation was a must, and they were just waiting in the wind for it to happen. A few people other than the young boys wanted to see Gahbe dead too. He owed a few old heads some money and was hesitant to pay, so if Tyrell didn't get the job done, someone else would.

A black Cadillac STS slowed to a stop and pulled to the curb. Wise Earl stepped from the driver's seat, hit the alarm, and walked into the projects. He spotted Six and the young boys as soon as he hit the strip, and then saw Tyrell leaning against the gate.

"Tyrell, let me talk to you for a minute," he said, as he approached the young hustler.

Tyrell looked around and followed Earl into the little park.

"Wassup, old man?"

"You hit the Italians, didn't you?"

"Yeah, and?"

"And? Tyrell you killed a kid."

"Yo, listen man, it is what it is. That shit is done wit'... everything good wit' you?"

Earl pulled a cigarette from his pack and lit it. The thought of that child being murdered for no reason was heavy on his brain. He couldn't stop thinking about it. "Hell no, everything ain't good. Look at me." He raised his shirt so Tryell could see the bandages.

"Damn... what the fuck happened?"

"It don't matter what happened. I'm bowing out the game. This shit is too much. My purpose for gettin' back in was to get rich, not shot."

"C'mon, old man, you know that's part of it. Look at my shit." Tyrell pulled his sweat pants halfway down and showed Earl his wound. "Niggas get shot... but life goes on. It's still money out here to get."

"Yeah, but it comes with a price. And that price is usually your life. I kinda wanna be livin' for the next twenty years. Not wearing a colostomy bag."

"So, what you sayin', old man."

"I'm sayin' I'm out. Done. Wavin' the white flag. I think I'ma start goin' back to church."

Tyrell burst out laughing. "Church? Yo, Six you hear this nigga? He talkin' bout he goin' back to church. You can't make no muthafuckin money in the church. Fuck is wrong wit' you, old man, you trippin'."

Earl didn't appreciate being clowned. "That's the problem wit' you young punks, you think you know every fuckin' thing, but you don't. I bet you didn't know the church is a billion dollar business."

"Fuck the church." Tyrell replied. "I know one thing, I hope you got that muthafuckin' bread you owe me."

"That's why I came." Earl reached into his pocket and pulled a roll of money out. "I'll see you wit' the rest in a few days."

Tyrell snatched the wad of cash from Earl's hands. Earl sensed the hostility, but he kept his cool and let it slide. He didn't come for a problem; he came to let it be known that he was stepping away from the streets.

Tyrell shuffled through the bills counting each one. "Nigga," he threw the money in Wise Earl's face. "You owe me fifteen stacks, what the fuck is that?"

"That's all I got right now. You see me, I'm fucked up."

"Fucked up?" Tyrell took a step forward. "I ain't tryna hear that fucked up shit, everybody fucked up. I'm fucked up... nigga jus' tried to kill me and you talkin' 'bout you fucked up." Tyrell was about to reach for his gun, but he had second thoughts. "Yo, Earl... get that to me, dog. I'm givin' you three days and I want my bread."

Earl got ready to say something slick, but didn't. He swallowed his pride and chose to be the bigger man, but inside he was boiling. He was fuming—ready to explode. Within those split seconds, he had envisioned himself whipping his knife from his pocket and jamming it in Tyrell's ribs. But he wouldn't get far. He wouldn't get but a few steps before Tyrell's entourage would pounce him like wild hyenas on a helpless prey. So he played the sucker role. "Three days... I'll have it for you, don't worry."

"I ain't the one that should be worried," Tyrell responded. "Now get the fuck outta here."

Earl shook his head, turned and walked off. When he walked past Six and the young boys Grasshopper had just come back from the store. He saw Earl had a cigarette in his hand and he wanted one.

"Yo, old timer... can I get cigarette?" Earl kept walking. "Yo! Old timer!" Grasshopper jogged to catch up with him. "Nigga, I know you—"

He touched Earl's shoulder and a spilt second later, his back was on the concrete and he was staring up at the clear blue sky.

"Oh shit! He knocked that nigga the fuck out!" Six and his crew started keeling over from laughter. But Grasshopper's little cousin didn't like that, and he wanted to do something.

Six saw him reaching for his gun and got up from the crate. "Hol' up, son, we ain't doin' that. That nigga an old school cat. Let 'em live."

"Let him live?"

"That's what I said. Do I need to repeat myself?"

The young boy dropped his head and walked off in the opposite direction. He wasn't about to challenge Six's authority.

"I can't believe you left my daughter back there wit' that fuckin' physco!" Priscilla banged the top of the dashboard with both hands.

"We'll get her back, don't worry."

"Don't worry? I want her back now!"

"We can't go back there, Priscilla. You killed a fuckin' cop!" Mox was doing 70 MPH in 50 MPH zone, swerving in and out if the congested highway traffic.

"How do we know he was a cop? He didn't show us a badge."

"Cop or not Priscilla... it's still a body. We gotta leave New York."

"Leave? I'm not goin' nowhere without my daughter. Pull over, Mox."

"I'm not stoppin' Priscilla. You buggin'."

When she saw he had no intentions on slowing down, she leaned over, grabbed the wheel and almost caused a major collision. Luckily, Mox was a skilled driver and was able to avoid a wreck.

"What the fuck is wrong wit' you, Priscilla? You tryna kill us?"

She impatiently sat in the passenger seat, tight lipped and furious. "Stop the car, Mox."

He ignored her and kept his eyes on the road ahead.

"Mox, stop the car and let me out. I'm not leavin' New York without Brandi. You can do what you wanna do."

"Priscilla, put your seatbelt on."

"Fuck the seatbelt, Mox. Stop the car!"

"The fuckin' police is behind us, put your seatbelt on."

As soon as Priscilla pulled the seatbelt across her chest, the cop hit the sirens.

"Fuck!" Mox looked at Priscilla and shook his head. "You see this shit..."

Priscilla turned in her seat to see where the cop was. "He's on us, Mox. You gotta go faster."

Mox checked the rearview and saw how close the patrol car was. "You gotta get 'em off me, Priscilla. They too close."

"What am I gonna do?"

"You still got bullets in that gun?"

Priscilla released her seatbelt, stuck her body halfway out the window, and aimed her gun at the police car. She squeezed the trigger and let three slugs fly from the barrel into the windshield. The window shattered and the officer jerked the wheel and swerved out the lane like he'd been hit by a bullet.

Mox maneuvered through a few more cars, hit the gas, and sped down the highway.

After driving for six and a half hours straight, Mox hit his right blinker and merged with the light traffic that was flowing off 95. He looked to his right and Priscilla was sleeping like baby—feet up in the seat with her knees to her chest.

Mox made another right turn onto West Broad Street, and kept straight until he saw the Hess gas station to his left. He tapped Priscilla's leg. "Wake up."

She squirmed in her seat for a moment and then wiped her eyes free of sleep. "Where are we?" she asked, looking around.

"Virginia," Mox answered. "Richmond."

"Richmond, Virginia? What are we doin' here, Mox?"

"I got a few people out here I used to deal with. I know we can blend in and move some of this work."

"What about Brandi?"

"We're gonna get Brandi back. Stop worrying. It won't do nothin' but stress you out. Lemme get things in order, and I promise we'll get her back." Mox cut the ignition and stepped out the car to go into the store. "You want somethin'?"

Priscilla shook her head no. She was still very upset at the fact that they had to leave their daughter behind. She couldn't believe it. She couldn't understand how someone could leave their child and be okay with it. It was disturbing her nerves.

On his way out the store, Mox's cell phone rang. His phone was new and he had given only a handful of people his contact information and the number that showed up on his caller ID wasn't familiar. He let it ring until it stopped, and then got back into the car. As soon as he pulled off, it rang again, same number.

"Why aren't you pickin' your phone up?" Priscilla asked.

"Because I don't know who it is."

"It could be Brandi, pick it up."

Mox thought about what she said. She could be right. He did make sure Brandi knew the number in case of an emergency, and this whole situation was an emergency.

He looked down at the phone ringing and finally picked it up.

"Hello?"

"Goddamn nephew, how many times I gotta call yo' ass before you answer... shit."

"I ain't know it was you Unc, wassup?"

"I need you baby, where you at?"

"I'm OT right now, but what's good?"

"Goddamnit!"

"What's wrong Unc, you got a problem?"

"A small thang, a small thang baby boy. But ahh... I need to see as soon as possible. When you coming back?"

"Gimme a few days and I'll meet up wit' you somewhere."

"Okay nephew, I'll see you then. Aye, listen, be careful out there. Keep your eyes open."

"Aight Unc, peace."Mox hung up and they pulled off.

TREMAYNE JOHNSON

CHAPTER ELEVEN

After one month of living in Virginia, Mox and Priscilla were right back in the game. This time; even deeper. Richmond was a foreign playing field they had to get familiar with, and even being slightly familiar, it was still a task trying to adjust, especially for Mox. But he intended to keep his cool and stick to his plan. It was only so much he could do without drawing attention to himself, so he chose to play incognito and shy away from the limelight.

On the other hand, Priscilla was slowly slipping back into some of her old ways. Somehow, she managed to befriend two females she was introduced to, and lately, she had been hanging out a lot. When confronted about it, her only excuse was, she missed her daughter and can't function without her.

Mox saw the switch in her demeanor when asked about it, but he didn't pay too much attention to it. The money was coming in steadily and he was ready to make his next move. Just a few more pieces had to be put in place, and everything would be all good; but everything's never all good.

Despite its vast population, Richmond, Virginia is a rather small, close-knit city. If something happened in north Richmond, the south and the west side would find out about it immediately. There was little that went unknown in the city, so when the word on the street was that a new face was in town; everybody knew whom it was—everybody but the one person who should have known.

———

Quiane and two of his partners relaxed on the posh sofas in The V.I.P area of Club Bliss. It was a Friday night, and as expected, the spot was jam-packed. A barrage of 6-8 women bombarded the V.I.P entrance with the hopes of someone spotting them and inviting them in.

Quiane glanced down the stairs at the small crowd of barely dressed women and shook his head. "Bitches do anything jus' to get in V.I.P."

"Ayo, that one right there with the blue dress on, she's bad." Kyle said. He was sitting to the right of Quiane, sipping his drink.

"That's Toya, I know them bitches." Kurt replied. He was sitting on the opposite side of Quiane going through his phone.

"Yo, Kurt... call 'em over here. I like that bitch in the blue, she can definitely get it." Kyle said.

Kurt was about to call for Toya, but Quiane stopped him. "Why every time we come to the club y'all niggas gotta invite these broke ass bitches to V.I.P? Fuck that... I ain't payin' for their drinks tonight. You niggas want 'em up here, y'all pay for their shit."

Kurt smiled at Quiane, stood up, and then pulled a roll of cash from his front pocket. "You ain't sayin' nothing nigga... I got money," He let the bills fall from his hand, and onto the table in front of them. "What's the price, my nigga? Two, three thousand?"

Hundred dollar bills covered the table. "We gettin' money, my nigga... this shit don't mean nothing to me, and it shouldn't mean nothing to you... ya' rich muthafucka."

"Yeah, and I wanna stay that way. I ain't trickin' on them bum ass bitches. Y'all niggas crazy." Quiane replied.

"It ain't trickin' if you got it." Kurt sang while pouring himself a drink. He tapped Kyle on the shoulder. "That bitch Toya a freak too, son!" he said, laughing.

"Oh word? Yeah, go get them bitches... fuck what this nigga talkin' about... I'm tryna score tonight."

Quiane shook his head at his homeboys and watched as Kurt made his move on the ladies.

On a regular night, Quiane would stop by Club Bliss, have a drink, and keep it moving. Tonight was different. Tonight, the club scene was a spectacle for all to see, and the entire city had come out to have some fun.

Looking down at the crowded dance floor from where he stood, Quiane watched the partygoers party hard. The music was blasting, clouds of fog filled the air, along with smoke from all the hookahs being smoked, and the women were coming in by the bunches.

Quiane finished his glass of champagne and thought he saw a face in the crowd that he recognized, so he started making his way down to the dance floor.

"Where you goin', nigga?" Kurt asked. He was coming up the stairs, followed by four women in tight dresses and mini-skirts.

"I'll be right back. I'm goin' to the bathroom." he lied.

By the time he reached the dance floor/bar area, the face he'd been looking for was mixed into the crowd of hundreds. It was almost impossible to find someone you thought you saw. He stood in the crowd and continued to survey the area.

———

Priscilla fixed her titties in her bra and then summoned the bartender. "Can I have a vodka with a splash of cranberry and pineapple, and two straight shots of Patron? What y'all drinking?" she asked her two friends.

"Same as you," they replied.

The downstairs bar area was overcrowded. It was only by a miracle that Priscilla and her girls managed to get some seats. Just as they were walking up, two men and a female were leaving, so Erin, the youngest of the three, rushed over and secured the three barstools.

Not even five minutes passed and they were turning down advances and free drinks from every dude that walked by. Priscilla's other friend, Ariel, was getting frustrated.

"Why every time we come to this spot, these weak ass niggas always pressin' us?" Just as she finished talking, a tall, light-skinned guy with curly hair brushed against her. He acted as if it were an accident, and then asked to buy her a drink.

"No nigga... I don't want you to buy me no drink," she said. "And you didn't get the memo, huh?"

"What memo?" he asked.

"Light-skinned niggas been outta style since eighty-eight!" The three women broke out in laughter while curly hair eased off to the next group of females. It was routine for the girls to turn down more than twenty guys in less than an hour, but after a while, it became irritating.

Priscilla downed her two straight shots of Tequila, tapped Erin on her arm and the two of them walked towards the bathroom. "We'll be right back, Ariel, gotta use the lil' girls room." she said, but Ariel knew the real reason for them going into the bathroom. It just wasn't something she was into.

"Okay, hurry up. I'll be right here."

When they got to the restroom, there was a line that almost stretched to the back exit. A hoard of scantily dressed women waited for their turn to use the bathroom.

"It's too many people on this line to be standin' around waitin'. C'mon, Priscilla." Erin snatched her friend's hand and they maneuvered their way to the front of the long line.

"Ungh Ungh bitch, I know you ain't cuttin' the line?" Someone shouted.

Erin and Priscilla kept it moving, and as soon as the restroom door opened, they slithered by the female exiting and scurried in.

"Damn girl... you gon' get us jumped in here." Priscilla wasn't used to Erin's way of doing things. She had an *I don't give a fuck, I'ma get mines'* attitude towards everything, and it seemed to be working for her, but Priscilla couldn't get familiar with it. It wasn't her style.

Erin was a true country girl from Tallahassee Florida. When she was 14 years old, her mother was diagnosed with pancreatic cancer, and 9 months later, she was dead. From that day on, Erin would learn to fend for herself. With no knowledge of who her biological father was, and her mother in a grave, she did what she felt was best for her. And what was best for her was the streets.

"Please... these bitches jus' be talkin'. They ain't gon' do nothin'." She pushed the stall door open. "C'mon... get in here."

Priscilla followed her into the stall and anxiously fiddled through her Chanel purse, looking for something. "I don't know where it is." She panicked, looking at Erin.

"Bitch, you better hurry up and find it. We ain't got all day."

"Oh, here it is." Priscilla pulled a piece of aluminum foil out, unfolded it, and sprinkled a tiny amount of the white, crystallized powder onto the back of her hand. Quickly, she shoved it up her nose and passed the foil to Erin, who did the same. When they finished, they washed their hands, fixed their hair, and made their exit.

On the way back to the bar, Priscilla felt someone tap her shoulder, but she kept walking. She knew how dudes in the club got after a few drinks, and she wasn't about to blow her high, arguing with some nigga. But once he grabbed her arm, she had to turn around.

"Get the fuck—" When she saw the smile, she could do nothing but laugh. She tried to remember his name as she stood there gazing into his eyes.

"Umm... umm..." She couldn't get it. "What's your name? I honestly forgot."

"You forgot, huh?"

"Yeah, I mean, it's normal to forget a person's name if you haven't seen them since the day you met them."

"So, you remember meeting me?"

"Yes. But I don't remember where. Enlighten me, please."

He smiled again and then looked at Erin. He'd seen her around before. "Quiane." he said, extending his hand to Priscilla.

"Yes. Quiane... now I remember. How are you?"

"I'm good, and yourself? I see you lookin' sexy as ever."

The compliment made Priscilla blush, which was rare. "Thank you," she replied. "I'm okay, just enjoying the weekend."

"Ughmm... excuse me," Erin butted in. "You not gonna introduce me to your lil' friend?"

"Oh... Erin, this is Quiane. Quiane, this is my friend, Erin."

"Why don't y'all come upstairs wit' me and my boys? We got drinks and everything."

Priscilla looked at Erin. "I can't leave my girls," she said.

"They can come too. Don't worry about it."

"Oh, y'all ballin' huh?" Erin joked.

"Nah, ma, we jus' like havin' fun... that's all. Now, y'all comin' or what?"

"Yes, we're coming. I just have to get my other friend. We'll meet you up there."

Priscilla and Erin rushed back to the bar area where Ariel was waiting.

"C'mon, we out!" Erin grabbed her arm and pulled her off the barstool. "We goin' to V.I.P."

"*V.I.P,* with who?"

"Priscilla's friend..." She tried to remember his name, but couldn't. "What's his name, Priscilla?"

"Quiane."

"Who?" Ariel didn't hear her.

"Quiane," she repeated. "I met him a while ago in New York. He helped me one day."

The three women looked up to the V.I.P area, and Quiane was staring down at them. He waved his arm in the air, telling them to come upstairs.

"Look, c'mon... " Erin pointed. "They're waiting for us."

Smiling, the three of them walked towards the stairs.

———

"Yo, Q... come here." Kyle was standing at the railing in the V.I.P overlooking the dance floor. "You see that nigga right there?"

"Who?"

"The nigga wit' the patch on his eye... right there."

"Yeah, yeah... I see him. Who is he?"

"That's the nigga I was tellin' you about. He out here gettin' money."

Quaine smirked as he peered down at the overcrowded club. He tipped the bottle of champagne to his lips and drank. After he wiped his chin, he looked at Kyle, and then over the crowd again. He wasn't too fond of new faces in his town, but tonight he was more focused on Priscilla. He'd deal with his new problem whenever he saw fit. "Get all the info you can on that nigga, and I'll take care of it on another date. Tonight," he said, watching the three women walk. "I'ma take care of this right here."

As soon as the girls reached the stairs that led to the V.I.P area, Ariel made a swift turn on her heels and started to go back downstairs. Priscilla chased after her to see what the problem was.

"Ariel, what's wrong?"

"Do you know who he is, Priscilla?"

Priscilla looked back. "Who?"

"Quiane."

"Oh, you know him?"

"Know him?" Ariel's eyes got big. "He's only *the* biggest drug dealer in Richmond. Duh... everybody knows him."

"And, what... that's a problem?"

"My boyfriend ain't gonna like the fact that I'm hanging out with his arch enemy."

"C'mon, jus' have one drink with us and then we'll leave."

"I can't, Priscilla... I gotta go."

Ariel didn't waste another second. She knew what Quiane was about. In fact, she had seen him and his cronies in action more than once. Richmond Virginia was her home, and she knew every player in the game. She also knew Quiane had a reputation for making trouble in the streets. It was something he liked to do.

"Where that bitch goin'?" Erin questioned, watching Ariel walk back down the steps.

"She said she had to go. Her man called."

Erin rolled her eyes and went back to the sofa where Quiane and his boys were sitting. She knew the real reason Ariel left, but she didn't care. Erin was out to enjoy herself.

Priscilla and Erin stayed in the V.I.P with Quiane and his boys for an hour. They had drinks, laughs and more drinks as they partied the night away.

Quiane and Priscilla were engaged in conversation the whole time. She could tell by the way his peers acted around him that he had power, and she knew he had a little bit of money from the watch he was wearing.

"That's a nice watch you got on."

Quiane smiled. "What you know about watches?"

"I know a lil' something. Not much, but enough."

"Enough, huh?" He smiled again, but this time Priscilla was blushing. "So, how you been Ms. Mysterious?" Quiane giggled.

"Ms. Mysterious? What's that supposed to mean?"

"It means exactly what it means. Listen, I saw you in need of help, so I helped you. But after I dropped you off, you got locked up and I never heard from you again. I would say that's kinda mysterious, wouldn't you?"

"First of all," Priscilla rolled her eyes. "You hit me with your fuckin' truck, so don't act like you did some Superman shit and saved the day." She bent down and grabbed at her leg. "I got the scar to prove it, too."

They laughed when Priscilla couldn't keep a straight face.

"I really didn't mean to hit you though. But you darted into the street like someone was chasing you. I always wanted to ask you what that was all about."

"Nothing." She replied nonchalantly.

"Nothing? It looked like something to me. You was runnin' for your life." Quiane laughed.

"Oh, that was funny to you, huh?"

"Nah, I'm sayin'..." he couldn't stop laughing. "You hauled ass up outta there."

"Well, all that's over and done with. I got new problems now."

Quiane sipped his drink. "Don't we all." he said.

For the next forty minutes, Priscilla and Quiane talked about everything that came up. They discussed life issues, and she badly wanted to let him in on her secret, but she was skeptical. She really didn't know this man, but she felt comfortable in his presence. It was something about the way he spoke. It was his aura—his swagger.

"So, where's your girlfriend?"

The question surprised Quiane and he almost spit his drink out. "*Girlfriend?* Who said I had a girlfriend?"

"Are you telling me you don't?"

"That's exactly what I'm tellin' you. What's good wit' you though... where's your man?"

"At home." she answered.

"Oh, so you do have one?" Quiane nodded his head. "He let you come out all sexy like that by yourself?"

"I'm not by myself... and he doesn't *let* me do anything. I do what I wanna do."

"I hear that. You a big girl, huh?" They laughed together.

In the middle of their conversation, Erin walked up sipping her drink. She nudged Priscilla on the arm and gestured for her to look downstairs. "We got trouble at twelve-o-clock," she warned.

At that moment, Priscilla had no idea what Erin was talking about; that was until she saw him with her own eyes.

"Oh shit." Immediately, she placed her drink on the table. "Sorry," she said, looking at Quiane. "We have to go."

Erin looked at her like she had two heads. "We?"

"Yes, we." Priscilla snatched her by the arm and tried to pull her towards the stairs, but Erin jerked away from her grasp.

"*You* gotta leave," she stated. "I'm stayin'. I'm enjoying myself, thank you." Erin rolled her eyes and took another sip from her drink.

"But we came together."

"Yeah, we did... but that's *your* man, so it's *your* problem."

Priscilla sucked her teeth and stormed off. She couldn't believe her so-called friend was acting this way, but there was nothing she could do. Erin had her mind made up, and nobody could tell her otherwise.

"Wassup wit' your girl," Kyle asked. "She good?"

"Yeah, she'll be just fine... her man downstairs."

"Her man, who that?"

Erin pointed to a table downstairs that was occupied by two guys. One of them had a shiny, baldhead and a patch over his eye, and the other had short, black hair and a pair of dark shades.

"Which one is her man though?"

"The one with the patch."

"Oh, word?" Kyle downed his drink and stepped over to where Quiane stood. He got close, leaned in and whispered in his ear. "You heard what that bitch jus' said, right?"

"Yeah... I heard." Quiane answered. "Send them niggas some champagne... it's time for us to get acquainted.

Mox crossed his left leg over his right knee, lit his cigar, and savored the sweet taste of the hand rolled leaf. He let the smoke out of his mouth and into a crowd of more than 200 people. The heavy bass thumped in his ears as he surveyed the jam-packed club.

"It's packed in here tonight," Travis said. He was sitting opposite Mox in a black Calvin Klein sport jacket. "I never saw it this crowded."

Mox nodded and continued to blow smoke in the air. With the overflowing crowd, he hadn't noticed the young lady creeping up on his left side, but Travis spotted her from ten feet away and gave him the warning.

"You got company."

Mox turned and saw Priscilla standing there with a half-smile on her face.

"You told me you weren't comin' out," she said.

"I changed my mind."

She rolled her eyes. "Yeah, now if I did that it would be a problem."

"It wouldn't be a problem. You do what you wanna do anyway."

"Please, Mox."

"Listen, Priscilla... I hope you ain't come over here to start arguing n' shit."

"I don't wanna argue with you, Mox. I came over to say hi." She reached down and gave him a hug and a kiss on his cheek.

"Excuse me, sir..." A female attendant interrupted. "Those gentlemen up there sent this to you." She placed a tin bucket filled with ice and a bottle of Moët Rosè on the table in front of them.

Mox looked up to where she pointed, but he didn't recognize the men standing against the railing. "You know them niggas?"

Travis raised his shades and peeked upstairs. "Yeah, that's the kid I mentioned the other day, Quiane... He moving a lotta weight out here heavy. He from up top though, I'm surprised you don't know him."

"Nah... I don't' know that nigga." Mox rubbed his chin. He couldn't understand why complete strangers would send over a $350 bottle of champagne. He puffed his cigar, let the smoke flow from his mouth, and slowly turned to Priscilla. She had a blank stare on her face—confused, like she was hiding something. "You know them niggas?" he asked, looking straight in her face.

"No."

Mox shook his head. He knew she was lying because she couldn't look at him when she answered.

"If you lying to me, you know I'm gon' find out. It's only a matter of time, Priscilla." he called the attendant who brought over the Moët and asked her what their most expensive bottle of champagne was.

"I believe it's the Remy Martin Louis the thirteenth."

"And how much is that, love?"

She pulled a small pad from the pocket on her shirt. "It's five thousand," she said.

Mox pulled three money stacks from a small black bag and passed one to the attendant. She ripped the band off and counted out five thousand in hundred dollar bills.

"Do me a favor." Mox picked up the bucket with the Moët in it and gave it back to her. "Send both of those up there with those guys, and tell 'em... if they gon' send something, make sure it cost more than a stack." He looked up at the three men and smirked.

"Priscilla, get your shit... Yo, Travis, let's get outta here."

CHAPTER TWELVE

Earl stood in front of the full body mirror and looked over himself. He was sharp as a tack. He placed his cufflinks on and straightened his tie. It was almost time to go, and he didn't plan to be late for his debut. He brushed some lint off his pants leg, checked his shoes, and then kneeled and said a prayer.

"God, I know you're up there watching down on us. Especially me..." he smirked and continued. "I jus wanna ask you for your guidance and support while I travel this long, tedious journey. Please, Lord, give me the strength, courage and wisdom to preach the word to the people. I know I haven't been the best person... but, I also know I'm not the worst. In Jesus name... Amen."

After a few moments of silence, Earl got back to his feet, snatched his keys and headed out the door.

Summer was withering away, and autumn was tapping on its front door. A cool fall breeze brushed past his face as he walked down the street to where his car was parked. Earls' stomach was in knots. The last time he felt like this was more than twenty years ago when he met his first wife, Estelle.

He jumped into the driver's seat, put the key in the ignition and slowly pulled off down the road. Twelve minutes later, he was parallel parking in front of Shiloh Baptist Church on Lincoln Avenue.

Earl turned the car off and sat for a moment watching all the churchgoers enter the House of the Lord. He thought about all the wrong he'd done; all the pain, heartache and misery he caused was slowly coming back to haunt him. It had been days since he had a good night's sleep. Physically he was drained, and mentally he was scrambled. His thoughts were a scattered mess. The demons he once suppressed were rising from the pits of his hell, and transforming his life into something that was becoming unstable.

A tap on the passenger side window interrupted his daze. He recognized the woman's face and rolled the window down.

"How you doin', Mrs. Bailey."

"Just fine, baby. Are you ready?"

"A little nervous, but I'm sure I'll be okay."

"All you have to do is let God guide you in the right direction. I see he got you this far. Leave all your worries to him. Don't even think about 'em." she replied.

Her kind, soothing words brought a tight smile to Earl's face. He was appreciative of Mrs. Bailey's encouragement, and felt it was just what he needed, so he stepped out the car and headed into the church.

As he walked up the steps to the front entrance, his stomach tightened and he felt queasy. Sweat built in his armpits and on his forehead. It had been years since his last church visit, and he had no idea what to expect.

He reached the door, and a small crowd of older women was lined up, entering the church one by one. Earl felt a hand on his shoulder and turned to see who it was. "Mrs. Garrett, how are you?" he asked, trying not to seem too nervous.

"Fine, and yourself?"

"Not too good," he said, laughing it off. "I think I'll be good... what you think?"

Mrs. Garrett smiled. She could see the sweat trickling down the side of his face. "Being nervous is natural, baby. You just go on in there and speak from your heart. God don't judge."

Earl agreed, and they walked into the church side by side.

Mrs. Garrett was one of the oldest sisters to attend the church, and she was also the one who convinced Earl to attend. After some much needed conversation, she was able to encourage him to share his story with the congregation.

When Earl stepped into the lobby, he signed the guestbook and an usher escorted him to his seat. Earl sat through the entire two and a half hours of service until they called his name. He closed the Bible he was holding, scooted past the two people sitting next to him and walked down the aisle to the pulpit.

He was dressed sharp in his new Brooks Brothers suit and matching wingtip shoes. The pastor stepped to the side and let Earl have the microphone.

Prior to him speaking, he scanned the crowd in hopes of seeing his nephew in attendance. The moment he realized there was no sign of him he immediately changed his mind. There was no way he could go through with his plan if Mox wasn't there.

"Umm..." his nerves were again getting the best of him, and the sweat was starting to reappear. "I had a few things I wanted to say to you all, but unfortunately, there's been a change in my plans. Forgive me for the inconvenience... I apologize."

As he stepped away from the pulpit, he noticed Tyrell standing at the back of the church. His stomach dropped and the sweat came down heavier. Earl was in debt to Tyrell, and he knew the only reason he was there was to collect. The problem was; he didn't have it.

Mrs. Garrett got up from her seat and went over to where Earl was. "What's the problem, baby?"

Earl shook his head. "It's not the right time, Mrs. Garrett."

"Okay baby... I guess the only time it's right is when God say it is. Until then, I'll keep you in my prayers." She moved to the side, and Earl hurried down the aisle. He had lost track of where Tyrell was in those few seconds, and he tried to rush out the door.

"Wassup old man, where you headed?" Tyrell asked, stepping out of a dark corner in the lobby.

Earl jumped at the sound of his voice and stopped dead in his tracks. He was terrified. "Ahh... ahh..." The words weren't coming out.

"I see you been playin' hide and seek, huh? This is what it's come to? This is what gotta happen for me to get mine? You owe me, Earl. I told you I want mine."

"Listen, Tyrell..."

Tyrell stared into Earl's eyes. The look was pure hatred. He eased his right hand underneath his shirt, but before he got the chance to retrieve his gun, Mrs. Garrett interrupted them.

"Tyrell, is that you?" she questioned, moving in closer.

"Yes, Mrs. Garrett." He answered, fixing his shirt.

"I can't believe how big you've gotten." She spread her arms and hugged him. Instantly, she felt the bulge on his waistline. "How's your mother? She doesn't come to the church anymore, is she alright?"

Tyrell knew she felt the gun, and he wanted to get out of there as fast as possible. "Yeah, she's fine Mrs. Garrett... thanks for askin'." He took a step towards the exit, but she grabbed his shoulder and whispered in his ear.

"You know God don't like ugly."

Tyrell looked at Earl, and then at Mrs. Garrett. He wanted to say something, but chose not to and just walked out.

CHAPTER THIRTEEN

"Fill it up... and keep the change." Mox told the attendant as he handed him a hundred dollar bill. He turned the radio down and removed the key from the ignition.

"Why you always come to this gas station?" Priscilla asked. She sat in the passenger seat with a pair of black Ray-Bans on, covering her swollen, red eyes, a tight short sleeve shirt, and a pair of fitted jeans.

"Because they have the best service, and it's the safest."

"The safest?"

"Yeah, you didn't notice there's always a patrol car or two at those other gas stations?" Priscilla shook her head no. "That's because you don't pay attention to your surroundings. You too busy doin' other shit."

"Whatever, Mox." she replied, sucking her teeth.

As the attendant finished pumping the gas, Mox's phone rang. He took a quick glance at it, looked at Priscilla, and then put the key into the ignition.

"Your phone is ringing."

Mox ignored her and continued to exit the gas station. When she went to reach for it, he pushed her hand away. "Don't touch my shit, Priscilla. We went through this before."

"So, pick it up," she said. "It's probably your lil' fuckin' girlfriend... what's that bitch's name?"

Mox was silent for a few seconds. He kept his hands on the steering wheel and his eye on the road ahead. "Priscilla, cut it out, alright. Every day you wanna start a fuckin' argument over nothing."

"Over *nothing?*" the phone was still ringing. "So why don't you pick the phone up? Because you know I'm right." As soon as she saw the opportunity, Priscilla reached over and hit the *'Answer Call'* button on Mox's phone and a female answered.

"Hello?"

Mox slammed on the brakes and almost caused a collision. He snatched the phone from the middle console and quickly hit the *'End Call'* button.

"What the fuck is wrong wit' you, Priscilla?" He tried to grab a handful of her hair, but she fought him off and swung an open palm that connected to the side of his face.

"I knew it was that bitch, you lyin' muthafucka!"

In the midst of their squabble, Mox was able to put the car in park. He jumped from the driver's seat, rushed over to the passenger side, and attempted to snatch Priscilla out of the car, but she was putting up a resistance that he wasn't expecting.

"I told you about puttin' your fuckin' hands on me." He struggled to pry her body from the vehicle, and the only thing stopping him was the seatbelt.

Priscilla tussled to stay on the inside of the car, but once Mox got the seatbelt loose, there wasn't much she could do.

"Mox, stop!" She cried as he pulled her hundred plus pound body from the automobile. Once he got her out, he dragged her through the middle of the street and onto a patch of grass.

"Why are you doing this?" she sobbed. "I love you... please... stop."

Mox was oblivious to her pleads and cries. "I ain't dealing wit' this shit no more, Priscilla."

Priscilla wiped the tears from her face and tried to catch her breath. "Why do treat me like this Mox? You know how much I love you."

Mox turned and started walking back to his car. He knew that what he was doing was absolutely wrong, but at the time, he felt there was a justifiable reason behind it. He loved Priscilla unconditionally—but the drama he could do without.

As he got closer to the car, her screams got louder. "Mox please, please don't leave me!" She jumped up from the grass, but by the time she reached the car, he was pulling away. Priscilla stood there in the middle of the street—withered, humiliated, and sobbing like a spoiled baby.

Ten minutes went by and she gathered herself and pulled her phone from her purse. She dialed a number and it rang several times. No one picked up, but less than a minute later, her phone rang.

"Hello?" she answered.

"Who is this?"

"It's Priscilla."

"Oh... hey, wassup baby?"

"Hey, I umm..." She was hesitant, but he was her only option. "I'm in a lil' dilemma and I need a favor."

"What is it, babe?"

"Can you come and get me?"

"Where are you, everything okay?"

Priscilla looked around for a street sign so she could tell him where she was. "I'm okay. I'm on the corner of Judah and Leigh Street. You know where that is?"

"Yeah, I'll be there in fifteen minutes, jus' stay there."

-FIFTEEN MINUTES LATER-

Priscilla found a shaded spot underneath a tree where she sat and cried until her eyes hurt. When she picked her head up, she saw a burgundy Jaguar pull up twenty feet from where she was. The passenger side window came down, and when she saw who the driver was, she began walking towards the car.

"Are you sure you alright?" Quiane asked after she entered the vehicle. He could see she'd been crying. Priscilla was mute. She wiped her face and shook her head no. Quiane wanted to ask what happened, but he knew it wasn't the right time, or the right place, so he turned the volume on the radio down low and drove off.

Two hundred feet away, across the street from a kids playing park, Mox impatiently sat in his car. His eyes were glued to the burgundy Jaguar and he had a strong feeling of who it was. He started the car when he saw them pulling off, and followed them at a respectable distance. While driving, he dialed Travis' number.

"Mox, what's good?" he answered.

"Ol' boy that was in the club... what he driving?"

"Umm..." Travis thought on it for a few seconds. "I saw him in a few different joints. Most recently a white drop, and a burgundy Jag... I think."

Travis had just confirmed Mox's suspicion. "Okay, cool."

"Why, wassup?"

"I got the drop on this dude. I'ma follow him for a minute and see what it is."

"Oh yeah," Travis laughed. "Be careful though, you heard? I'll see you later."

CHAPTER FOURTEEN

Cleo was out of breath as he stood over the wounded man, sweating, clutching a hot pistol in the palm of his right hand. "You got one more chance to tell me where that money is, or it's over for you," he said.

The victim, a 25-year-old young black male by the name of Jamal was lying face down on his living room carpet. His hands were rope tied behind his back, and black electrical tape covered his eyes while faint sobs and pleas for help escaped his lips. The bullet hole in the back of his right thigh was leaking blood all over the rug. Jamal was silently praying for God to spare his life.

Since migrating south, Cleo figured he'd try his hand in the drug game. That only lasted a few months before some stick-up kids kicked his front door in and robbed him of everything but his life. He was able to escape a tragic situation by the skin of his teeth, but that particular incident is what made him take a different turn in his career choice. It wasn't long after that, he started robbing the drug dealers himself. In his mind, it was easy money. Much easier than selling the drugs, because all he had to do was find a potential target, plot on him for a few days, and then attack.

The change in occupation was lucrative. Cleo had more money then he'd ever had, and was feeling like he was on top of the world.

"Turn over, nigga!" He kicked Jamal in his left rib and he rolled onto his back. "All you gotta do is tell me where it is, Jamal... you makin' this real difficult."

Whoadie, Cleo's partner, was tossing the house, looking for anything he could find—money in particular. So far, he had come up with nothing. After ransacking the closet in the master bedroom, he lifted the mattress on the king sized bed in hopes of finding something underneath—but he came up empty handed again. He stood in the middle of the bedroom looking around. He knew something was there, but he just couldn't pin point it. His eyes searched the room for the tenth time, and then fell upon the painting that was hanging over the headboard of the bed. It was slightly crooked and looked out of place.

Whoadie jumped on the bed. As soon as he touched the painting, the right side fell down, revealing a hidden safe that was built into the wall. "Jackpot." he mumbled, and then called for his partner. "Yo, Cle!"

Cleo was still towering over Jamal, continuously kicking him in his stomach and ribs—so much that he threw up the previous night's dinner. He looked up when he heard his name. "You found something?"

"Yup!" Whoadie was examining the safe, trying to figure out how to get it open. It didn't have a keypad or any visible locks. He jumped off the bed and ran downstairs to where Cleo was. "I found the safe." he said.

Cleo's eyes got big and he smiled. "I knew there was something in here. You been playing games wit' me all fuckin' night." He raised his leg and stomped on Jamal's testicles. "What's the combination, muthafucka?"

Jamal grunted in pain but never once screamed. He hadn't said a word since they entered the house. He knew if they were lucky enough to find the safe, they wouldn't be able to open it unless he was there—alive.

Cleo bent down and shoved his pistol in Jamal's mouth. "Stop makin' this so hard, and give up the combo."

"Yo, Cle..."

Cleo ignored Whoadie. He was too focused on obtaining the combination to the safe.

"Yo, Cleo!" he yelled.

"What, nigga?"

"Ain't no keypad or lock on that joint... Go check it out."

Cleo looked down at Jamal. His lip was busted and blood was trickling down the side of his mouth.

"You gon' make me kill ya' stupid ass, Jamal." He turned around and ran up the stairs to the second floor where the master bedroom was.

As soon as he entered the room, his eyes went straight to the safe. He jumped on the bed to get a good look at it, and it didn't take long before he figured out what he needed to open it. He rushed back downstairs.

"Pick this nigga up," he told his partner.

Whoadie struggled for a moment, but eventually got Jamal to his feet. "What you want me to do wit' this nigga?"

"Bring his ass upstairs... he gon' open that safe for us."

They dragged Jamal up the stairs and Cleo had him stand on the bed in front of the safe. He ripped the electrical tape from around his eyes, grabbed his neck and shoved his face right into the safe. After holding his head there for ten seconds, a green light appeared at the top of the safe. Jamal wasn't even putting up a fight. He knew it was over. There was nothing he could do.

Cleo wrapped the tape back around his eyes and then pulled a knife from his pocket and cut the rope that was tied around his wrist. He snatched Jamal by the arm and placed his right hand onto the handprint that was on the safe. Ten seconds later, another green light came on and the safe opened. Before seeing the contents of the safe, Cleo shoved Jamal off the bed and emptied his clip into his back. The shots echoed throughout the moderately furnished home, but no one for at least a quarter mile would hear them.

"Empty this shit and let's get outta here." On their way downstairs to leave, Cleo heard a key enter the front door lock. "Oh shit... go back, go back." He whispered as they darted back up the stairs and into the master bedroom.

The front door opened and then closed, and a female shouted, "Jamal!"

Cleo and Whoadie panicked. "Why the fuck you didn't tell me somebody else would be here with him?"

Whoadie looked confused. "I didn't know," he whispered back. "Every time I came here he was by his self."

The female shouted again, but this time, her voice was getting louder because she was walking up the steps.

"Yo..." Cleo whispered. "She's comin' up here. Stand on that side."

They stood on opposite sides of the door, so in case she decided to enter the room, she wouldn't be able to see them immediately.

Cleo gripped his pistol. He quietly released the empty clip and pushed a full one into the bottom of the weapon. The only thing they could do was wait.

The footsteps were getting closer and closer.

"Jamal, I just had the most stressful day at work... ughh... I'm starting to hate my job," she said. "Jamal?" she checked the bathroom. "You in there, babe... I had to arrest this young black kid today.

Cleo's eyes bulged at the word *'arrest'*. He looked at Whoadie. "This bitch is a cop?"

Whoadie looked even more confused. He just shrugged.

The doorknob of the bedroom turned and the female cop entered the room. The first thing she saw was the painting on the wall. It was leaning to the left, and the safe was wide open—emptied of its contents.

She rushed over to the bed and almost tripped over Jamal's bullet riddled corpse. She immediately went to reach for her service weapon.

"You touch that gun, you gon' be layin' next to him." Cleo said. He had his weapon aimed at the female cop's head.

Once she turned, she saw the two men standing there, pointing guns at her. "Put those guns down guys... c'mon, let's not do this the hard way."

"Shut the fuck up, I'm givin' out orders 'round this muthafucka." Cleo replied. He took two steps towards her, holding the gun with both hands.

"She's a cop Cle... we need to get outta here." Whoadie suggested.

"Listen to your boy, Cle..." she said, repeating his name. "Put the guns down and walk out of here. I'll act like I never saw anything."

"You must think I'm stupid, huh?" Cleo took another step towards the officer, raised his pistol, and slapped her on the side of her face with it. "Lay the fuck down!" he demanded.

She stumbled into the dresser, holding her cheek. Blood oozed from her nose, through her fingers, and down her hand as she pleaded for her life. "Please don't do this. I'ma cop... you'll never get away with this."

Cleo glanced at his partner and then down at the female officer. He hated cops. He hated their uniforms and everything they stood for. Never did they protect and serve—only harass and arrest. He held the gun tightly in his sweaty palms—itching, anxious to take the shot. He took a deep breath, looked directly into the eyes of the female officer, and shook his head. "Wrong place, wrong time." he mumbled.

The shot burst forth and the first slug ripped into her shoulder, pinning her to the carpet. She collapsed and landed right beside Jamal.

Whaodie followed suit and squeezed the trigger on his weapon, releasing hot lead into her chest cavity. Her body jerked and shivered each time a bullet entered her. After the third or fourth slug, she was dead and blood was seeping from every hole in her body.

"Whoadie, let's make a move!" Cleo shouted. The two shooters dashed from the house and into their car that was parked out front.

They hit the highway and drove 30 miles without saying a word. When they felt they were in the clear, smiles danced across their faces.

"This shit is too easy," Cleo expressed. "It can't get no easier than this." he looked over to his partner. Whoadie was smiling, but he wasn't as excited as Cleo. "What's the problem?"

"Man... we jus' killed a cop, Cle... that's serious shit. You know we can't go back there... ever."

Whoadie was right and Cleo knew it. "Be easy man... we good. Fuck it, we jus' go somewhere else. It's niggas gettin' money all over the globe. Fuck you trippin' for?"

"I ain't trippin' nigga... I'm jus' sayin'... where the fuck we gon' go?"

Cleo turned and glanced at the duffle bag in the backseat. "I'm pretty sure we got enough money to go where ever the fuck we wanna go."

Whoadie sat quietly in the passenger seat. He was thinking hard. "Oh," he said, sitting up in his seat. "My cousin."

"Your cousin who?"

"Remember I was tellin' you about my family from up top... the nigga, Quiane."

"Oh, yeah... the fly, pretty muthafucka."

"Yeah, him. He in Virginia gettin' it, I spoke to him a few days ago."

"Oh word," Cleo kept his hands on the steering wheel, but his mind was in Virginia. "So, call that nigga and let him know we on our way."

"Aight." Whoadie replied.

TREMAYNE JOHNSON

"But yo... what part of Virginia is he in?"

Whoadie rubbed his chin, trying to remember the city his cousin was staying in. "Umm... hol' on... oh, I think he said Richmond... yeah, Richmond Virginia, that's it."

"Richmond huh?" Cleo pressed the gas harder and the speedometer reached 90 MPH. "I bet there's a whole lotta niggas gettin' money in Richmond. Fuck it... Richmond it is."

CHAPTER FIFTEEN

-SOMEWHERE IN NEW JERSEY-

A stint of light coming from the flickering flame atop the candle on the television stand was all that could be seen. The rest of the room was pitch-black. The scent of sweaty sex was prevalent in the air and the sounds of repetitive moans filled the atmosphere.

"Yeah baby, ride that... show daddy you know how to work the stick." Priest was lying on his back in his plush king sized bed, holding onto the slim waist of his young companion, while she bounced on his hard dick.

"Ooh... I feel this dick in my stomach daddy... ooh!" April arched her back and slid up and down Priest's rock hard shaft until she felt her climax building up. She licked her lips, pressed her chest against his and shoved her tongue in his mouth. They exchanged hot saliva for a few seconds, and then she kissed his neck and went down to his chest. When she flickered his nipple with her tongue, he jumped from the pleasure. "You like that?" she asked.

Priest moved his hands from her waist and palmed her ass cheeks. "Yeah, stay on that dick... jus' like that." he moaned.

April slid up and down a few more times, and slowly slid off.

"Whoa... whoa, what you doin?" He tried to grab her ass.

"Shhh... I got this," she whispered and slid between his legs. She pecked his hard-on with her soft lips. "You like that?" Priest nodded yes. April cupped his balls with her left hand, stroked his shaft with her right, and slurped on the head of his dick like it was her favorite Blow-pop.

"Oh shit, I'm 'bout to come, baby." Priest's body tightened up and he exploded in her mouth.

April didn't budge. She swallowed every drop that came out, looked up at Priest, licked her lips and smiled.

Suddenly, the bedroom light came on. "Bravo! Bravo! Encore! Encore!" Two white men in suit jackets, jeans, and boots stood at the bedroom entrance, clapping as if a show had just ended.

"What the fuck!" Priest shoved April off the bed, rolled over to the opposite side and went to reach for his gun underneath his pillow, but he was too slow. One of the agents rushed over with his weapon drawn and put the barrel to the tip of Priest's nose.

"Reach for it, I dare you," he said, gripping the weapon tight with both hands. "Get the fuck on the floor."

Priest slowly eased his hand away from the pillow and took a deep breath. These guys sounded like cops, and if the sounded like cops, more than likely they were.

"Aight... don't shoot, jus' chill." Priest begged, sliding off the bed. He lay flat on his chest with the side of his face pressed against the hardwood floor.

The second guy in the suit jacket came over to where Priest lay. "Get up," he said, kicking his leg. "It's time you and I have a conversation." He turned to April, who was crouched in the corner covering her naked body. "Here, put some fucking clothes on." He tossed a t-shirt at her.

Priest got up slowly. He was butt naked, standing face to face with the guy in the suit jacket. "Conversation? I don't even fuckin' know you."

A quick, sharp right hand connected to his lower abdomen and he went down to one knee.

"Good, because I didn't tell you my fucking name yet, smart ass. Now, listen here, Mister Priest. We can do this the easy way or the extremely hard way. Your choice."

Priest raised his head and glanced at the other guy in the suit jacket. He still had his gun in hand. He weighed about 220 and stood over six feet, which made him slightly bigger. Priest contemplated a rumble with the two men, but he honestly knew that he didn't stand a chance. He understood the end result would not be a good one.

"What the fuck you want?" he questioned, holding onto the spot where he got hit.

The white dude in the suit jacket reached inside his pocket and pulled out a badge. He tossed it at Priest and it hit his chest and fell to the floor. "I'm Agent O'Malley, and that's my partner, Agent Havoc.

Priest turned and glanced at Havoc. He was still clutching his weapon. "I ain't did nothin' for the Feds to be fuckin' wit' me." he said.

Agent O'Malley grabbed a pair of pants that were on a chair in the corner of the room. "Here," he said, tossing them at Priest. "Put the pants on and we can talk."

Priest slid into the jeans and then fished for his tank top that was hidden underneath the covers. Once he found it, he put it on. "So, wassup?"

Agent O'Malley pulled the chair up to the bed and faced Priest. "We got you on an attempted murder of a federal informant, but I think we can work something out."

Priest smiled, showing his pearly whites. He didn't believe a word that came from O'Malley's mouth. In fact, he was starting to think they weren't even cops. "Fuck outta here," he said. "Y'all fuckin' buggin'. I didn't attempt to murder anyone, you got the wrong person." He went to stand up, but O'Malley pulled his piece from his waistline.

"Sit your black ass down before I put a bullet between your fucking eyes."

"Aight, chill." Priest put his hands up and sat back on the bed. "I'm tellin' you though, you got the wrong person. Whatever you talkin' about, I didn't do it."

"So, who the fuck is this?" O'Malley whipped out a picture of Earl lying in a hospital bed.

Priest swallowed the lump in his throat. "I don't know that nigga."

As soon as the last word rolled off his tongue, O'Malley's right palm was connecting to the side of his face. "Don't fucking lie to me!" he yelled.

Agent Havoc stepped up and pushed his gun in Priest's face. "Let me shoot this piece of shit, O'Malley."

"Stand down, Agent."

"Wait..." Priest was regaining his equilibrium. "Wait... aight... hol' up." He touched his jaw because it felt like he got punched instead of slapped. He looked at O'Malley's hands. They were huge. "Aight, I know that muthafucka, but he ain't no federal informant."

"You sure about that?"

"Man, that's Earl. I known that nigga all my life, and I ain't never heard of him being a rat."

"Yeah, well certain circumstances will make a person do things they normally wouldn't do."

Priest looked around the room. April was still crouched in the corner. "I ain't no snitch."

O'Malley glanced at Havoc and laughed. "Don't they all say that in the beginning?" He got up from the chair and stood over Priest. "Listen asshole, I know more than you think I know, believe me... but our problem ain't with you."

"So, why you fuckin' wit' me?"

"Shut up and listen," O'Malley demanded. "This little attempted murder situation, this is nothing. You'll do what, ten... fifteen years. Not to mention this is fed time, not that state shit you did before." He sat back in the chair. "You too old to be going back to jail, Priest. Help us help you."

Priest sat in silence for a moment. Out of all the crimes he'd committed, and all the times he's been interrogated, never once had he been asked to cooperate. It was as if they knew he wouldn't do it, so they never asked. Priest was a stand up dude, and as far as he knew, so was Earl. That's why it was hard to believe what O'Malley was saying. "I don't know about this..." he said, rubbing his head. "It jus' don't sound right. Why the fuck would Earl be workin' for the Feds?"

O'Malley pulled his cell phone from his pocket. "Earl done got himself into something he can't get out of." He passed the phone to Priest. "You know him?" It was a picture of Tyrell.

"Nah." Priest lied again.

"That's Tyrell Michaels. We got him on a murder charge and a few drug cases. Young muthafucka thinks he's Nino Brown or something." O'Malley shook his head. "Anyway, Earl owes the kid some money and hasn't paid yet. Word is Tyrell put some money on his head."

"And being that you guys have this information, you went to Earl with it, and he's willing to help y'all if y'all help him, correct?"

"Exactly." O'Malley answered.

"So, what I got to do with this?"

"I'm getting to it, I'm getting to it." O'Malley took the phone from Priest, moved to the next picture, and handed it back to him. "There's our problem, and I'm pretty fucking sure you know who that is." It was a picture of Mox.

"Nope."

O'Malley used his other hand and slapped the opposite side of Priest's face. "You keep lying to me and I'll keep fucking you up."

Priest felt his cheek and smiled. It didn't matter how many pictures they showed him, the answer would always be no.

"Now, here's what it is..." O'Malley stood up again. "Our only concern is him right there," he pointed at the phone and then to Priest. "Your son. Your one and only biological son, Mox Daniels."

Priest took a deep breath and dropped his head.

"C'mon Priest, we know everything. Earl's sister's murder on down to Mox's little brother's murder... even Brandi's kidnapping... all of it." O'Malley scooted the chair closer to the bed, leaned in to Priest's ear, and whispered. We even know that it wasn't you who killed Mox's mom. Believe me Priest, we know every-fucking-thing."

Priest closed his eyes and fell back onto the bed. He couldn't believe how much information they had.

"Help us help you, Priest... do the right thing." Agent Havoc instructed.

"We want Mox and Priscilla, Priest. Bring them to us and all this will go away."

Mox sat up, wiped his face and chuckled. "I guess y'all don't know everything, huh?"

"What's that?" O'Malley asked.

"How you expect me to get close to Mox, when he thinks I murdered his mother. He wants to kill me."

"Don't worry about that."

"Don't worry about it?"

O'Malley was getting upset. "Yeah, what are you hard of fucking hearing now? I said don't fucking worry about it." he reached down, picked up his badge and holstered his gun. "Let us worry about everything else, you just bring them back here."

Priest was confused. "Bring them back, from where?"

"Richmond, Virginia."

Priest scratched his head. "Y'all want me to go to Richmond, Virginia, find my son and his girlfriend, and bring 'em back to New York, so you can lock 'em up?"

O'Malley tapped Priest shoulder. "There you go... see, you're picking up quick."

"Suck my dick, you cracka muthafucka. I ain't doing—"

Those were the last words Priest got out, before Agent Havoc smashed him in the back of his head with the butt of his service weapon.

"What the fuck did you do that for?"

Agent Havoc shrugged. "Fucking guy kept talking smack, O'Malley. How much of that shit am I forced to listen to?"

"Goddamnit!" O'Malley kicked the chair. "We didn't get him to say yes."

Agent Havoc stared at Priest knocked out on the bed. "I bet his ass say yes when he wakes up."

They laughed. "Aye, you..." O'Malley called to April. "Get dressed and get the fuck out of here. Don't ever let me see you around this fucking piece of shit again."

April snatched her belongings and dashed out the house half-dressed.

"Aye, Havoc... you got a real fucking grudge against black guys, huh?"

"Leave it alone, O'Malley." Havoc knew exactly where his partner was trying to go with that remark.

"I'm just saying... your wife still banging that drug dealer guy?" O'Malley burst into laughter.

"Fuck you, O'Malley."

"Yeah, try going home to fuck your wife, asshole."

CHAPTER SIXTEEN

"Damn Unc, I hear you... stop yellin' in my ear." Mox replied, holding his cell phone in one hand and the steering wheel in the other.

"Well, I'm jus' makin' sure, nephew. How long before you get here?" Earl asked on the other end.

"I'll be through in like twenty minutes. I'm starving too... been driving all fuckin' night." Mox turned his lip up and side eyed Travis, snoring in the passenger seat. "I should'a stopped in Harlem and got something to eat, but I said fuck it, I'll jus' get somethin' when I get there."

"I got food here, don't worry."

"Aight Unc, I'll see you in a few." Mox hung up and continued north on the highway.

The sun had just come up and the highway was empty of traffic. Mox pushed the rented Porsche truck to 80 MPH, clutching the steering wheel, and at the same time keeping an eye out for lurking law enforcement. They were known to be hidden in certain spots off the road—camouflaged—waiting to catch someone moving above the speed limit.

"The Glamorous Life," by Sheila E came on the radio, and Mox raised the volume above 10. Travis squirmed in his seat, trying to get all the rest he could, but Mox had different plans. The loud music wasn't enough, so he tugged at Travis' arm and rolled all the windows down. The fresh November winds smacked his face and he jumped to attention, wiping his eyes, looking around.

"Wake up, nigga. We in New York."

Travis looked at his watch. It read ten minutes past 6 am. "Damn nigga," he said, stretching. "You was flyin', huh?"

"Hell yeah. I did ninety the whole way."

It was a few minutes past midnight when he and Travis got on the highway in Virginia. Due to the light traffic, he'd been able to make the trip in one of his fastest times yet.

Travis slipped his sneakers back on and sipped his water. "I know one thing, I'm hungrier than a muthafucka. I hope we goin' to get somethin' to eat."

Mox agreed. "Me too. You already know. My uncle said he got some grub at the crib, so we good."

They cruised the remaining distance until exit 16 came up and Mox veered to the right and got off.

As far as Mox and Priscilla's relationship, the past month and a half had been rough. The strain was beginning to put distance between them. Priscilla would come in at the wee hours of the morning several times during the week. Mox knew what it was, but he didn't want to let go, and neither did she.

Mox's trips to New York became more frequent, and were no longer strictly business. More than often, he would be mixing his business with his pleasure, and he knew better than to be doing that.

Despite the altercations and all the drama, Mox was still seeing Jasmine. Only now, it had become more normal and serious. He purchased a three-bedroom condominium in Hartsdale, New York, and she was living in it. Jasmine was satisfied, and for the time being, they lived a drama free life, but those moments don't last long.

"When was the last time you was in New York?" Mox asked Travis.

"Shit... I ain't been back here since I was six years old."

"Damn, that's a minute. Your family ain't out here?"

Travis gazed out the window at his birthplace. "Nah, my mother didn't have any brothers or sisters, it was jus' us. Once we moved south, she never looked back. I don't know who my father is..." Travis paused. "Fuck that nigga... and my grandmother died five years ago."

"Yeah, I be feelin' the same way. You know what's real though?"

"What's that?"

Mox tightened his grip on the steering wheel and glanced at Travis. "I jus' hope my daughter don't say that shit about me."

The rest of the ride to uncle Earl's house was silent. They pulled up to the address he had given them and Mox parked the truck. He turned the engine off and snatched the key out the ignition.

"This your uncle's crib?" Travis asked.

Mox shrugged. "I guess so. This is where the GPS brought us. I never been to this spot. He do so much moving around, you never know what this dude is into."

The property they were in front of was a one family townhouse style home with a short driveway and a small front yard. Mox and Travis got out the car and walked to the front door, but before he got a chance to knock, the door opened, and uncle Earl was there to greet them.

"Nephew, wassup?" he said with open arms.

"Whaddup, Unc." Mox hugged him, patted his back, and got a good look at him. "You lookin' good Unc... I see you," he said, smiling.

Earl looked at Travis. He'd never seen him before. "Who's your homeboy?"

"That's my road dog, Unc, Travis," he answered.

Earl extended his arm and shook Travis' hand. He pulled the door all the way open and let the two men inside.

"So, what's the emergency, Unc?" Mox looked around the nicely furnished house. His uncle always had a good sense of style.

Earl took a seat on his brown leather couch and picked the Bible up off the coffee table.

"Did you ever read this book, Mox?"

"Bits and pieces. Why?"

Earl opened the Bible to a page he had bookmarked and recited a passage to himself. After he finished, he looked up at Mox. "This is the most powerful book you could ever read. You know why?"

"Nah, why?"

"Because it can change your life, Mox." Earl looked down at himself. "I'm livin' proof, nephew. I found my calling... and this book right here is the reason."

Mox had a stunned look on his face. "I don't understand where you going wit' this, Unc. What, you read the Bible... okay."

Earl shook his head. "You don't get it, nephew," he tried to explain. "I found God, Mox. I accepted Jesus Christ into my life, and ever since that day, I pray and worship him every minute of every hour. I thought you were gonna be here a few weeks ago, and I had something set up. I need you to come to the church with me."

"To the church?"

"Yeah, next month, on Christmas Day. I'm getting baptized and I want you to be there. I also got a few words to say."

Mox stared at his uncle to see if he was joking or not, but Earl kept a straight face. "You serious huh?" he asked.

Earl nodded yes. "Excuse me for being rude. Y'all want something to drink?"

"Yeah, get us some water, Unc... and bring some food."

Earl went into the kitchen to fix some drinks and a few snacks for his houseguests while they sat and relaxed on the couch. Almost ten minutes went by before he returned, carrying a tray with two glasses of water and two plates of food.

"Yo, Unc your phone was ringing, somebody named O'Malley called." Mox said, pushing the cell phone to the other side of the table.

Earl's eyes popped wide open at the mention of O'Malley, but neither Travis nor Mox caught it. "Yeah, umm... that's the guy from the church. I'll give him a call back in a few."

The deception was making Earl extremely uncomfortable. This was his nephew—his bloodline. And although he hadn't snitched on him, he was still a rat because he was going to snitch on someone else. He knew how Mox felt about rats; in fact, the most important rules of the game he learned from Earl. But circumstances were different now. Tables were turned, and the cards that were dealt were now being played. Earl was still coming to terms with the decision he made. He felt it was best for his well-being. He was afraid for his life.

"So, Unc," Mox broke off a piece of the grilled cheese sandwich and tossed it in his mouth. "You really gettin' baptized, huh?"

"Yeah nephew, this serious. I need to make a change in my life style. I need some stability—some direction."

Mox listened to every word his uncle said, and he sounded sincere. It was the first time he'd heard him speak about religion with such passion. "I respect it Unc, shit... I got no choice but to respect it, but you already know how I'm living. I really don't do the church thing."

"You tellin' me you not coming?"

"Nah, I'm not sayin' that. I'll be there, don't worry."

Mox and Travis sat with Earl for an hour before they left. Hartsdale, New York was one of the few stops he had to make before going to see Juan Carlos to handle his business.

-HARTSDALE, NEW YORK-

Mox hit the lights and slowly pulled into the gated community. He punched his code in the panel at the front gate and continued up the winding road until he was at his front door.

A black Mercedes Benz and a blue Corvette occupied the two guest parking spaces next to Jasmine's Range Rover, so he knew she had company. He parked a few spaces down and he and Travis got out the car and walked to the house. Before he stuck the key in the door, he could hear the music playing loud from the inside. "They probably in there drinkin' n shit." he said to Travis as he opened the door.

Mary J Blige and Lil' Kim's video, "I Can Love You," was playing on the flat screen television and blasting through the surround sound. Jasmine's two friends were in the middle of the living room dancing and singing along.

"Y'all havin' a party, huh?" Mox said.

Jasmine looked up smiling. She knew her man's voice anywhere. She lowered the music video and got up from the sofa to greet Mox. "Wassup babe?"

He wrapped his strong arms around her soft, warm body. "You miss me?"

Jasmine kissed her teeth. "Nope," she joked, kissing his lips. She reached down and cuffed his sack. "I miss him, though."

"Yeah? I bet you do." Mox looked at her two friends. "Wassup Melonie?" He had no idea who her other friend was, so he just waved. "Jasmine, this my homie Travis. Travis this my boo, and her crazy ass friend, Melonie."

"How you doin?" Travis shook Jasmine's hand and waved at her two friends.

"Are you staying for dinner, Mox?" He wanted to say yes, but time wasn't permitting him. He had a couple more stops before his meeting.

"Nah, babe... I told you, I gotta take care of something. Next time I come up, I'll be able to stay."

No was exactly what Jasmine didn't want to hear. She told Mox that she was comfortable with their situation, but honestly, she was jealous of Priscilla. She was annoyed at the fact that he constantly expressed his love for her, but woke up every morning to someone else. Jasmine no longer wanted to be viewed as second in line; she wanted the top spot. But to even be considered for that spot, she needed a relevant explanation—a sure reason for him to leave the person he was with.

"Mox, I need to tell you something." Jasmine grabbed his arm and led him into the kitchen fifty feet away.

"I'll be right back," he told Travis. Once they entered the kitchen, Jasmine grabbed the lump in Mox's pants and massaged it. She got close to him and slipped her tongue in his mouth. Mox cupped her ass cheeks as he felt his dick hardening. "Chill... you gon' get him hard," he whispered in her ear.

"That's exactly what I wanna do." She whispered back, pulling his zipper down. Jasmine started to go down on her knees, but Mox stopped her.

"Not right now babe... I told you, I gotta go."

"Shh..." She put her finger to her lips. "It won't take long. I got you." she assured.

Mox couldn't resist seeing her soft, wet lips around his hard dick. Jasmine gave the best head. It was one of the many reasons he kept going back. And he agreed with her. The way she worked those lips, it wouldn't take long at all. Seconds later, he succumbed to her sweet seduction. He leaned his back against the seven-foot refrigerator and let Jasmine take control.

She released his medium hard-on from his boxer briefs and let it fall over her hand. Jasmine loved chocolate, but she loved Mox's chocolate pipe even more. She licked her lips at the sight of his muscle hardening in her grasp, kissed the tip, and then took as much in her mouth as she could.

The music came back on, and Mox jumped and turned to see if anyone was coming. Jasmine kept sucking. She held his stiffened manhood in both of her hands while she slobbed on his sack.

"Relax baby," she said, jerking and sucking his shaft. "They're not coming in here, we're alright." Her motions sped up and Mox let his head rest against the refrigerator. His eyelid shut, and felt his climax building up. Minutes later, he opened his eye and watched Jasmine with her pretty face, slob all over his dick. She stopped and looked up at him. "Am I doing it good, baby?" Mox nodded yes. "I want you to cum in my mouth, and all over my face." Mox nodded yes again. He couldn't seem to get any words out of his mouth.

Jasmine continued stroking Mox's long, log like, third leg. He snatched a handful of her hair once he felt his nut coming and she kept her lips wrapped around his head.

"Ooooohh... I'm cummin' baby."

Jasmine opened her mouth wide, and got ready for his load to shoot down her throat, and Mox exploded. She jerked faster, catching everything that came out. It was in her eyes, dripping off her chin, and even in her hair. "Damn baby, that was a lot." She said, wiping cum from her face. "I still haven't told you what I need to tell you."

Mox smiled. "I thought this is what you needed to tell me?" He looked down at his dick.

"Part of it," she answered. "But not the most important part."

"Important part, what's that?"

Jasmine snatched a paper towel, wet it, and then wiped her face clean. She was hesitant on revealing the news to Mox. She didn't know how he would react, and the last thing she wanted to do was push him away. She gazed into his eye and tried to read his thoughts.

"You know I love you, right Mox?"

Mox smiled. "I love you too." he replied.

"You know I understand our situation, but to be honest, I want more of your time."

"Babe, I can't—"

"Wait," she cut him off. "Let me finish saying this. Mox, I haven't been with a man that made me feel this good in a long time. I can honestly say that I trust you, I love you dearly, and I want us to start a family together." She paused and waited for his reaction.

Mox was silent. He didn't know what to say. He loved Jasmine, and had strong feelings for her. But for them to start a family, they would have to make a child, and that was something Mox hadn't planned.

When she saw he wasn't going to say anything, she blurted out. "Mox, I'm seven weeks pregnant."

"You what?"

"I'm seven weeks pregnant," Jasmine grinned. "We're gonna have a baby."

"A baby?"

"Yes Mox... a child, you know... an infant. How does that make you feel?" Mox was stunned. He didn't know whether to be happy because of the blessing or upset because of his situation. "Well, say something."

"I guess I feel good," he paused. "Yeah, I feel good... I mean, there's a life growing inside of you, how can I not be happy?"

"So, you're not mad?"

"No," he said, wrapping her in his arms. "Not at all. It's a surprise, but it's also a blessing. I'm very happy that you're carryin' our child."

"You being happy makes me happy, Mox." She leaned in and kissed his cheek. "I love you and there's nothing that can make me change the way I feel."

"I love you too, babe. Listen, I got some important business to take care of, so I gotta get outta here. I'll call to check up on you and make sure you all right. Cool?"

"Yes," she answered. "But I would be much better if you stayed."

"You know I can't stay, baby. Next time I come up, I'll stay for a few more days than I usually do, how's that?"

"I don't have a choice, do I?"

Mox shrugged and kissed her cheek. "I'll see you in a few weeks." Before walking out, he looked in her eyes and placed his hand on her stomach. "Take good care of our baby," he said, before he and Travis made their exit.

CHAPTER SEVENTEEN

After visiting Jasmine, Mox floored the $90,000 vehicle up the highway to New Rochelle. It had been months since he walked through the projects. The memories served as horror stories that he felt he could live without. His reluctance was built mostly on fear; he was afraid to face his reality and deal with the issues at hand, he kept dodging them— eluding the truth, running from his own shadow.

He tapped the blinker on, got off at the exit and navigated his way through the back blocks and onto Webster Avenue. Once he reached Horton Avenue, he parked, and he and Travis got out the car. "This is my hood, this is where it all started."

It was two days before Thanksgiving and the hood was empty. A cool breeze whizzed by and blew some leaves into the street as the two men entered Hartley Projects.

"I know that ain't that nigga, Mox!" Someone shouted.

Mox and Travis turned their heads at the same time, trying to see who was speaking, but no one was on the street; just parked vehicles. Mox saw someone wave their arm out the window of a red Mercedes Benz three cars from where they stood.

"Who that?"

"Come and see!" he yelled back.

Mox looked at Travis and began walking towards the parked car. When he got within ten feet, he heard the door pop open and the driver stepped out.

"Whaddup nigga?" Tyrell threw his arms up.

"Oh shit, Rell... whaddup?" A smile came across Mox's face. He han't seen Tyrell in almost a year. The last time they spoke, it was about Dana's murder. "Okay, I see you lil' nigga." he nodded. To see Tyrell doing good for himself brought joy to his heart. He could tell by his demeanor and the car he was driving what type of business he was into, but Mox never judged anyone. "You got your weight up, huh?"

Tyrell smiled. He had a certain respect for Mox. He knew everything he told him was to benefit him in the end. In the short time they did spend around each other, Tyrell soaked up plenty of jewels. He learned a lot and saw a lot. "Yeah, something like that." he answered modestly. "I'm jus' out here tryna eat like everybody else."

"Trying? Mox smirked. "Stop frontin', nigga, I see you... new Benz n' shit," He pointed to the car Tyrell got out of. "You fresh, probably fuckin' all the bitches... I know nigga."

Tyrell laughed. "Yo, chill... you wild." He pulled a roll of money from his pocket and held it up so Mox and Travis could see it. "Fuck them bitches, though, this is what it's all about."

Mox was impressed. The young boy was coming into his manhood. "Take a walk wit' me real quick." he said. "Oh," he turned to Travis who was standing off to the side. "Yo, Rell, this my homey Travis. Travis, this my lil' homey Rell."

"Peace." Tyrell gave Travis a pound. "C'mon Mox, we can walk up the block." He turned and yelled down the block. "Yo Six! Yo Six!"

"Yo!" Six screamed from sixty feet away.

"Keep ya' eyes open!" Tyrell shouted and then tapped Mox and they walked off. "So, what's good?"

"Wassup wit' the white boys?"

"Them niggas is history. I handled that."

"You handled that, handled that?" Mox repeated.

"I handled that, my nigga. Trust me, newspaper clippings and all." Tyrell reached into his back pocket, pulled his wallet out, and showed Mox the newspaper clipping. He took a few seconds to read it through. The only light on the street was from the street lamps, and he had to squint to see the words on the paper.

"You killed a kid, nigga."

Tyrell dropped his head in shame. Out of the many things he'd done in the street, that was something he wished he could take back. "I didn't mean to do it. I thought he was gonna stay inside.

That's my word, Mox... that shit be fuckin' wit' me too."

"What about Vinny? I don't see anything about him."

"I don't think he was there, and if he was, he was inside."

Mox didn't like the fact that a kid had been killed, but he was satisfied. Mikey and his brother were dead, and if need be, he would deal with Vinny when the time came.

"Have you seen or heard from Frank or Nate?" Mox asked.

Tyrell dropped his head again. "You don't know, huh?"

"Know what?"

"The Italians hit Nate in Frank's club a couple months back."

"Get the fuck outta here..."

"Word."

Mox couldn't believe it. "Not Nate, Nate was tough as nails."

"They caught him slippin'... fuckin' wit' them bitches in the club and not payin' attention to his surroundings."

"Damn," Mox shook his head. "So, where the fuck is Frank?"

"Shit... I don't know. Police shut the club down and nobody ain't seen that nigga. Like he disappeared off the face of the earth."

"Dissapeared, huh?" Mox laughed. "Yeah... so, wassup? You wanna make some real money?"

"What's real money?" Tyrell asked.

"A hunit... hunit and fifty a day."

"Every day?"

"Every day."

"You tellin' me I can make a hunit thousand dollars every day of the week... even Sunday?"

"Nigga," Mox paused and looked Tyrell in his face. "Even on Sunday."

The headlights from a dark colored car at the stop sign up the block caught Tyrell's attention. "Watch this car comin' down," he warned. "Niggas ain't gon' catch me slippin'." He pulled his gun off his waistline and cocked it.

Mox took a few steps back, between two parked cars, and watched as the vehicle cruised down the street. It seemed to slow up once it reached Tyrell, but then it kept cruising by.

"Them niggas come back around this block, they gon' get it."

Mox looked down at the gun in Tyrell's hand. "You can't get money and be out here on some gun ho shit... it ain't gon' work."

"It's been workin'."

"How long you think that's gon' last? Not long at all. A few more months and you'll either be dead, or locked away for the rest of your life."

"Mox, I ain't tryna hear this shit right now. I'm out here. Any nigga disrespect me or mines, and they gettin' it. Straight like that. I ain't got time to be playin' wit' these niggas."

"And that's exactly what I'm tryna tell your hard headed ass. You wastin' your time out here, you could be livin' like a king if you wanted to."

"I'm already livin' like a king," Tyrell flashed the Oyster Perpetual Rolex on his wrist. "This ain't no regular nigga shit. Grown men can't even afford the kind of shit I be rockin'."

Mox chuckled. He had no choice but to respect the youngster. He was holding his own. "I see you, and I also see you ain't gon' change your mind, but that's cool."

"It ain't broke, Mox. You know as well as I do, If it ain't broke, don't fix it."

Mox agreed. "You right." He gave Tyrell a pound and he and Travis walked to the truck.

"What that lil' nigga talkin' about?" Travis asked.

Mox started the car and pulled off. "He doin' his own thing; I respect it though, I can't be mad at the lil' nigga, he getting' a lil' money so he feelin' good... fuck him."

The next morning, Mox and Travis met up with Juan Carlos in the Bronx so they could handle their business. As instructed, the Porsche truck with

worry about how she would get Brandi back. Her only concerns were money and drugs.

For the past few weeks, Priscilla and Quiane had been seeing each other more than often. She started catching feelings for him—something she vowed not to do. She also understood that the consequences of her actions could be deadly.

When she was with Quiane, she was happy. She felt wanted and appreciated, loved and connected; desired.

Quiane was smart, handsome, and to top it off, he had a lot of money—lots of money. His nickname on the streets was, The Million Dollar Man, and some say that was just being modest.

Born and raised in New York, Quiane was the youngest of his brothers. His mother was a retired school teacher who devoted herself to church, and his father had just come home from a twenty year bid in the Feds for drug trafficking.

Quiane was introduced to drugs as a child, and ever since then, it's the only living he's made.

Everything he ever got and anything he has now, came from drug money.

He owned a $300,000 five bedroom mini mansion that he had built from ground up on three acres of land in Highland Springs. It contained all the amenities of the most lavish homes in the area. An indoor/outdoor swimming pool, a professional sized tennis court, a gymnasium that housed a basketball court, and a 17 hole mid-sized golf course. It was a drug lord's lair—the king's castle.

Priscilla relaxed in the Jacuzzi with her hair tied up in a bun, wearing a one piece Christian Dior bathing suit. She popped a strawberry in her mouth and took a sip of her mimosa as she smiled, watching Rhianna's music video on the flat screen television mounted to the wall.

She felt the presence of someone else in the room and she immediately turned to see who was there.

"Gotcha!" Quiane shouted, popping out from behind the door. He was holding a bouquet of pink and white roses in one hand and a bottle of champagne in the other.

Priscilla almost jumped out of her skin. "Boyyy... don't be scaring me like that. What's wrong with you?"

Quiane laughed. "I'm sorry. You looked a lil' bored in here, I was tryna liven you up."

"Liven me up with some of that," she replied, pointing at his dick.

Quiane bent down, kissed her lips, and handed her the roses. "If I didn't have this business to take care of, I would have no problem doing that. But wait until later... I'ma come back and wear that ass out."

"I'm not gonna be here later."

"Why not, where you goin'?"

"Quiane, it's Saturday. I'm pretty sure my man is back at home. I don't want any problems and I do not wanna hear his mouth."

"Oh, that nigga. Fuck that nigga." Quiane didn't like Mox one bit. He barely knew anything about him, but the fact that Mox had something he desired was enough. "Tell him you was with me and see what he say."

"Yeah, right." Priscilla stepped out of the Jacuzzi, snatched a towel off the rack, and started drying off. "You tryna start trouble."

"That's something I'm good at," he said. "Oh, I forgot... you don't want your little boyfriend to get hurt."

"Fuck you, Quiane."

He laughed. "I must have struck a nerve, I'm sorry."

"Kiss my ass."

"Bend over."

"Grow up, okay. You're fuckin' forty years old and yet you still act like a child. "

"I'm acting like a child, but you're the one keeping secrets from your man. You might as well tell him. Sooner or later he's gonna find out. I jus' hope he can accept it."

"Accept what?" Priscilla questioned.

"Accept the fact that I have his bitch now."

"*Bitch?*" She rolled her eyes. "Ain't nobody's bitch here, you better go find one of them hoodrats. You got me confused, boo boo."

"So, why haven't you told him?"

"Because he doesn't need to know." She shot back.

"How about I tell him? I would love to see his reaction." Quiane reached for Priscilla's arm, but she pulled away and started walking out the bathroom.

"You know... sometimes you say the lamest shit," she mumbled.

"What you say?" Quiane caught up to her.

"You heard me."

Slap! His right palm met the side of her face. She grabbed her cheek in shock; surprised that Quiane had put his hands on her.

"Watch your fuckin' mouth when you talk to me."

Priscilla stood there in a stupor—speechless and unsure of how to react. A tear slid down from the corner of her eye, but she wiped it away before it reached her cheek. Her thoughts were scrambled and she was confused. She believed Quiane was different, but she'd been proven wrong; he was just like the rest of them.

"Priscilla! Priscilla you here?" Mox yelled as he stepped through the front door. The house was quiet and didn't smell of food, so he knew she wasn't cooking. "Priscilla!"

"Yes! I'm upstairs!" she answered. She took her time coming downstairs because she had a pounding headache from the slap that Quiane had given her earlier. She even missed the bruise on her face when she checked herself in the mirror, but Mox caught it.

"You miss me?" he asked, holding two Gucci shopping bags in his hand.

Priscilla smiled when she saw the bags. Gucci was one of her favorite stores to shop in, and Mox knew it. "Just a lil' bit," she said, showing him the amount with her fingers.

"Well, that ain't enough," he responded, hiding the bags behind his back.

"Pleeeease..." She begged, getting closer. Priscilla wrapped her arms around Mox's neck and pecked his lips.

"What the fuck happened to your face?" he questioned, seeing the light bruise on her cheek.

Priscilla's eyes widened and her instinct caused her to touch the exact spot where the bruise was. "Huh, what?" She acted as if she didn't know what he was talking about.

"What you mean, what? You put your hand right on it." Mox's mood switched. "Don't fuckin' play wit' me, Priscilla."

"Mox, I don't know what you're talking about." She lied, and rushed over to the mirror that was next to the front door. "Where? I don't see anything."

Mox shook his head and dropped the bags on the floor. He knew she was lying and he was fed up with her dishonesty. He was tired of the falsehood they were living in—the backbiting, deceit and deception. It was time to come clean; time to lay all the cards on the table and man up. Time to tell her the whole truth.

"You fuckin' him, ain't you?"

An eerie silence swept the entire house. Not even the sounds of nature could be heard. Priscilla turned to Mox with a confused look on her face. "What are you talking about, Mox?"

"You know what the fuck I'm talkin' about, Priscilla."

She tried to laugh it off like it was nothing. "You buggin, Mox."

"Oh, I'm buggin... I'm buggin', right?" Mox pulled his cell phone from his pocket, went through his pictures, and held it up to Priscilla's face. "Tell me I'm buggin' again and watch what the fuck I do to you."

Priscilla's bottom lip dropped when she saw the picture of herself and Quiane getting out of his car and getting ready to walk into his house. "Mox... I..."

"Shut the fuck up. You tell another lie and I'ma—"

"I didn't fuck him, Mox."

"Stop lying to me, Priscilla. You was in there for three hours. What the fuck you doin' in that niggas house for three hours?"

"He only gave me a ride home, Mox, I swear." Tears started to build up in her eyes. "I swear he only gave me a ride because you left me. I didn't have any other way to get home."

"Three hours, Priscilla?" Mox smiled, but inside he was crying. "You stayed at that nigga's house for three hours and you expect me to believe that y'all ain't do nothing? You lied to me that night in the club and said you didn't know who he was. " Mox stood in the middle of his living room looking around. He had just purchased the house with cash, over a hundred thousand in cash. "All this shit," he said, waving his hand. "I did it for you... for us, and what you do? You go behind my back and fuck wit' some lame ass nigga who probably sold you a dream."

"For me?" Priscilla was livid. "Fuck what you did for me, Mox. Where's Brandi, huh? Where's our daughter, Mox? Oh, did you forget that you had a daughter? Don't fucking stand here and criticize me like I'm the only one who did some fucked up shit in this relationship." The tears came pouring out of her eyes. "You did me wrong, Mox, and you know it. I loved you and you did me wrong. You told me you

loved me. What this fuckin' tattoo we got, " she pointed at her neck. "I guess this shit don't mean nothing, huh? I thought it was let no one stand before we... before us Mox, you and I. You don't love me, you jus' say that shit to appease me."

"I do love you, Priscilla."

"No you don't!" she screamed. "You don't continue to hurt the person you love. You don't do that, Mox."

Mox knew she was right, and there was nothing he could say. The only thing left to do was to tell her everything. Tears were falling from Priscilla's eyes like a waterfall. She could barely catch her breath. "Priscilla..." Mox called her name and she tried to ignore him. "Priscilla, look at me."

"What, Mox?"

"Jasmine's pregnant."

CHAPTER NINETEEN

"You sure this the right address?" Cleo asked.

"It gotta be. This is the address he gave me."

Cleo pulled up to the trailer home and parked in the grass. It looked abandoned. The small, shack like trailer was rundown and dilapidated, but there were two cars parked in front. He snatched the key out the ignition. "Well, go see if he's in there." he said to Whoadie.

Whoadie stepped out the car, walked to the door, rang the bell and waited. He could hear people shuffling around inside.

"Who is it?" A female asked from inside the trailer.

"It's Whoadie, is Q here?"

The locks came off and the door opened. Standing in the doorway was a short, brown skinned female who was naked from the waist up. Her breasts were perky, her hair was in a ponytail, and she had a white dust mask over her nose and mouth. "He back deer," she said, in a heavy southern accent.

Whoadie turned and waved to Cleo who was still standing by the car. "C'mon," he told him.

The trailer home had very few pieces of furniture; a table, a couch and some chairs. Four half-dressed women sat around the mid-sized wooden table, sifting cocaine, cutting it, and placing it in plastic lunch baggies.

"Ladies..." Cleo greeted, smiling from ear to ear.

He and Whoadie were escorted to the back where Quiane sat on a twin-sized bed, tossing stacks of money into a black duffle bag that was on the floor.

"Cousin, what's good wit' you?"

"Same shit, looking for a come up. What's good wit' you?"

Quiane smiled. "Who's your boy?" he asked, ignoring Whoadie's question.

"This my nigga, Cleo."

"What's good?" Cleo extended his arm to shake Quiane's hand.

"What y'all niggas doin' in Richmond? Ain't shit out here."

"Came to see you."

Quiane looked at his cousin and smiled again. "Nigga, what the fuck you did?" He knew his cousin's only reason for being there was because something happened.

"I didn't do nothing I wouldn't usually do. You know how I get down, boy."

"Yeah, " Quiane nodded. "I know exactly how you get down. I need a favor though."

"Anything for you cuz, what you need?"

Quiane pulled a piece of paper out of his pocket and passed it to Whoadie. "Drop this bag off at the address and bring the other bag back. Can you handle that?"

"I got you, cuz."

Quiane tossed two more stacks of money into the bag and pushed it towards Whoadie. When they got back out to the car, Cleo jumped in the driver's seat and Whoadie put the bag in the trunk and then got in on the passenger side.

"How much you think is in the bag?" Cleo asked, starting the car.

"I don't know... couple hunit thousand prolly."

Cleo thought about the amount of money in the bag. They already had over a hundred thousand in cash, two guns, and some jewelry from their last robbery, but he wanted more. He was greedy and never satisfied.

Before they reached the address that Quiane gave them, he pulled over to the side of the road. Whoadie looked around; he was confused. "Why you stop? This ain't the address." They were on a dirt road surrounded by thick woods on both sides.

"I gotta check that tire on your side. I think it has a leak." He lied, grabbing the gun that was underneath his seat. Cleo got out the car and walked around to the passenger side. He bent down to act like he was checking the tire, and when he came up, the gun was in his hand and it was pointed at Whoadie.

Whoadie tried to duck, but the bullet crashed through the window and hit him in his ear. He was slumped over the middle console with blood coming from the hole in the side of his head. Cleo put two more slugs in his chest to make sure he was dead, and then opened the door, dragged his limp corpse from the vehicle, and left him the woods. He then continued to the address that was on the paper.

Cleo rang the bell, and as soon as the door was opened, his gun went off. Flame shot from the barrel and several shots followed. The other two occupants of the house tried to scurry to safety, but Cleo was swift. He moved through the small trailer, clutching the pistol, pumping lead into any moving figure in his sight. When the shots stopped, there were three dead bodies spread throughout the trailer.

He looked around. The setup was identical to Quiane's with a table, chairs and a couch. When he walked into the kitchen, there was a duffle bag that looked exactly like the one Quiane had given Whoadie. He unzipped it and smiled. It was full of cocaine. With both bags in his possession, Cleo got back into his car and drove off.

THE NEXT DAY

"This ain't like my cousin, he don't do shit like this." Quiane explained. He got up from the chair he was sitting in and paced the floor. Kurt and Kyle sat on the sofa directly across from him, and Priscilla was walking in from the kitchen. "Kyle, did you get in touch wit' Tammy?"

"Nah, not yet," he answered. "I called a few times but no one answered."

Quiane rubbed his hands together, trying not to think about the worst case scenario. "I know somethin' happened... yo, y'all niggas take a ride over to Tammy's spot and see what's up. Call me as soon as you get there."

"How much was in the bag, babe?" Priscilla inquired.

"About, two hunit."

"And you trusted him with all that money?"

"It was times I gave him more than that. I know my cousin. Whoadie don't get down like that. I been around him all my life..." Quiane paused and collected his thoughts. "That nigga he was with though... I don't know about him."

"Who was he?"

Quiane tried to recall the name. "Umm... I don't know. I forgot what Whoadie said his name was... fuck!" he yelled.

"Calm down babe, we'll get to the bottom of it... trust me." Priscilla massaged his shoulders and then sat in his lap. "The last thing you need to be stressin' over is money, we'll get it back."

"It ain't the money I'm worried about, it's the product. The only place I can get high quality product like that is in New York, and right now, I can't go back up there. I gotta take care of this shit down here."

"Can you get someone else to go up there?"

Quiane thought about it. "Nah, Kurt and Kyle got warrants in damn near every state, so I can't ask them to do it. Besides them, I don't trust no one else."

"I'll do it for you." Priscilla said.

Quiane stared her; she wasn't smiling, she was dead serious. "Do what?"

"I'll go to New York and handle whatever you need me to do. I'm capable."

Quiane grinned, but Priscilla kept a straight face. "You serious ain't you?"

"Why wouldn't I be? I mean, it can't be that hard of a task, right?"

"You don't even know what you gettin' yourself into. This shit ain't no game, Priscilla. You can get fifty years doin' this." Quiane explained.

"Can I ask you somethin'?"

"Yeah."

"Do you love me?" Priscilla asked, looking directly into Quiane's eyes.

"Yeah, I love you."

"Do you trust me?"

Quiane hesitated. "Until you give me a reason not to."

Priscilla brushed the side of his face. "Quiane," she whispered. "If I give you my heart, would you protect it with your life?"

"Of course I would, Priscilla." Quiane leaned in close, kissed her lips and she kissed him back.

"So, let me do this for you."

Before he could answer, his cell phone rang. "Hello?"

"This shit is ugly, Q... blood everywhere, no bags, and no sign of your cousin, Whoadie."

"Fuck!" He slammed the phone on the carpet, took a deep breath, closed his eyes and tried to figure out a solution.

Seconds later, when his eyes opened, Priscilla was standing directly in his face. "All you gotta do is tell me who I need to see."

CHAPTER TWENTY

Mox hadn't heard from Priscilla in almost a week. He was starting to believe that it was over for them; their relationship was finished. He felt in his heart the he had done the right thing by exposing the truth and telling her what it was, but never did he think she would leave. He loved Priscilla dearly and would do anything for her. But to wait in the wind for her to come back from who knows where, is something he wasn't going to do.

"What if she comes back and you gone?" Travis asked, watching Mox put the last bag into the car.

"That's her problem. I'm goin' back to New York. Christmas is two days away, Jasmine is pregnant, and my uncle Earl is gettin' baptized."

"What about the work that's on the streets?"

"You take care of that. Handle it how you see fit." He snatched the last of his belongings and piled them into the rental car. "I'ma see you when I come back, Travis... and keep my muthafuckin' house clean too." he said, laughing and jumping into the driver's seat. Right before he put the key in the ignition, his cell phone rang. "Hello?"

"You have a collect call from an inmate at a Westchester County Correctional Facility. To accept this call, please press three. If you no longer wish to receive..."

Mox pressed three and cut the recording short. He had no idea who it was, but he wanted to find out. "Hello?" he repeated.

"Yooo, Mox what's good... it's Bing."

"Bing, what's good boy... damn nigga, they got you again?"

"Yeah, man... serious shit this time. Them alphabet boys snatched me up two weeks ago. I had just moved out here to White Plains n' shit... I was chillin', but I guess they had other plans. These muthafucka got me in the federal hold up here in

Valhalla."

"Damn son, so what you need? You know I got you." Mox asked.

"I'm good right now. Only thing I need you to do is get a message to my sister. She stay over there by the old Yankee stadium."

"I got you."

"Good looking, Mox, I appreciate it. You know how we do."

"Aight Bing... hold your head, peace." Mox hung up the phone, started the car and pulled off.

-NEW ROCHELLE, NEW YORK-

"I told you I was going to get yo' punk ass." Tyrell cursed. "Six, bring that nigga over here."

Gahbe was naked as a newborn baby, shivering and shaking in the winter frost. It was so cold that the tears and snot coming from his eyes and nose was freezing on his face. Six held him by the back of his neck and walked him to the edge of the roof where Tyrell was standing.

"Kinda cold out here huh, Gahbe?" Tyrell joked. "Check this out though... I'ma give you an ultimatum. Either you can jump off this muthafuckin' roof by yourself, or you can take the bullet that gon' come out this pistol."

Gahbe's hands were shaking as he wiped the snot from his face. "Fu... fu... fuck you nig... nigga. Ki... kil... kill me mutha... muthafucka!" he spat.

Tyrell grinned and glanced at Six. "This nigga talkin' big shit, huh? Move Six." He pulled a black.9-millimeter from his coat, cocked it, walked up on Gahbe and pressed the barrel against his forehead. "I'm startin' to like this shit Gahbe... you know... this murder shit. You should'a killed me when you had the opportunity, you bitchassnigga." He stared into his eyes and squeezed the trigger. The echo from the blast was heard throughout the entire projects, and Gahbe's body fell to the pavement.

-CHRISTMAS DAY 2012-

Mox woke up at 5am Christmas morning. He

brushed his teeth, showered and got dressed to go out and get an early breakfast. Light snow flurries fell from the clouded skies blanketing the cold pavement as he cruised the empty streets of New Rochelle.

After a light breakfast, Mox went to pick Jasmine up so they could get ready to attend church services. It was a special day. A special day for Mox because it would be his first time in a church in years, and a special day for his uncle, Earl, because today he would turn over a new leaf and begin a new life.

While they sat in the car at a red light, Jasmine stared out the window at nothing in particular. She was in a deep trance. She rubbed her stomach and thought about the life that was growing inside of her. She thought about starting a family with Mox, and a smile appeared on her face. It was all she ever wanted; all she ever longed for.

Right before the light turned green, Mox's cell phone rang. He looked down at it and saw it was Priscilla calling, so he picked it up. "Hello?"

"I'm in New York, Mox, I wanna see you."

"For what, Priscilla?" As soon as Mox mentioned her name, Jasmine's head turned.

"Because I love you, Mox, and I want us to be together."

"You shoulda thought about that before you started fuckin' around on me."

"We both did wrong, Mox. Let's put the past behind us and move forward."

"I am movin' forward."

"What about our daughter? You jus' gonna leave us in the wind like we ain't shit?"

"You were fine without me before, you'll be alright. I gotta go." He said, trying to get her off the phone.

"Mox wait..." Priscilla sniffled. "Are you going to church for uncle Earl's baptism?"

"Yes, Priscilla."

"Will you talk to me, please? I jus' need to say a few words to you, that's all. I think you owe me that."

"Owe you?" Mox looked at Jasmine in the passenger seat. She had a disgusted look on her face.

"Listen... Priscilla, I gotta go. Bye."

Agent O'Malley and Agent Havoc pulled into Priest's driveway. His car was parked in the garage, so they had a strong feeling that he was home. They hadn't heard from him since their visit, and they were highly upset because he hadn't followed their orders to find Mox and bring him to them.

They exited the vehicle and walked to the front door. After banging for two minutes, Agent Havoc decided to walk around the house to see if the back door was open. He checked the knob and to his surprise, the locks were off, so he called to his partner. "O'Malley, I got an open back door over here!"

O'Malley walked around to the back of the house and they slowly pushed the door open. The stench was atrocious. Both agents covered their mouths and rushed out the door.

"What the fuck is that smell?" Havoc yelled.

"Smells like somebody got to Priest before we did.

Shit... C'mon, let's go back in and find him."

"Fuck no! I'm not going back in there, that shit is horrendous." Havoc complained. "If he's dead, what the fuck we going in there for? Call the coroner."

"Stop being a pussy and get your ass in here."

The two agents searched the house for Priest's body. They found him in his bathroom, slumped in his tub, with a bullet hole in his head.

"Oh my God, I think I'm gonna throw up." Havoc turned around and hurled on the floor.

"Jesus Christ, Havoc... get it together.' O'Malley said. He stepped inside the bathroom covering his nose and mouth and looked down at Priest's decomposed corpse. "Probably been in here a few days... fuckin' guy stinks."

"What's that?" Havoc asked, seeing a note sticking to the mirror.

O'Malley ripped it off the mirror and read it.

They could never say I wasn't a stand up nigga. Tell Mox I didn't kill his mother, and I love him.

———

Earl killed the ignition and stepped from the vehicle. He had ten minutes before church would start and he was nervous as hell. He wiped the beads of sweat from his forehead and walked up the stairs and into the church.

"Good morning, Earl." Mrs Garrett greeted. "You ready?"

Earl nodded and continued into the church. It was packed. Since he'd been coming to the church, he'd never saw it this crowded. The whole neighborhood attended. He scanned the crowd looking for the people he invited. He saw Mox sitting in the front row next to Jasmine and smiled. He knew his nephew wouldn't let him down.

Earl also spotted Tyrell and Priscilla in the crowd, and thought he saw someone who had a striking resemblance to Cleo. He took a deep breath and walked down the aisle to the pulpit. Dressed in his best suit and shoes, Earl was ready to let the truth be told. The congregation quieted and when he stepped in front of the microphone, he cleared his throat and began.

"Good morning ladies and gentlemen, and merry Christmas to all. Today is a very important day for me. Not just because it's a holiday, but because this is the day that I rejoice and confess my sins." He paused, looked over the crowd, and continued. "I've done a lot of good, but there's one thing I can't seem to erase from my brain, and that's the murder of my sister." Earl looked down at Mox sitting in the first row. "I think I owe my nephew an apology."

Mox didn't understand what his uncle was trying to say. He just listened.

"I been living a lie for thirty years, and I can no longer live like this." Earl placed his hand on the Bible and closed his eyes. "If we confess our sins, he is faithful and just, and will forgive us our sins and purify us from all unrighteousness."

Mox's heart dropped when he heard his uncle Earl reciting the prayer. It was the same prayer that the killer said the night his mother was murdered. He stood up and stared at Earl standing in the pulpit.

"I'm sorry, Mox." A tear fell from his eye and

splashed the Bible. "I'm sorry for taking my sister's life, I'm sorry for lying to you... I'm sorry for everything. I hope you can forgive me." Earl stepped back from the pulpit, reached for his waistline and pulled out a black.38 revolver. Before anyone could react, he put the barrel of the gun to his temple and hugged the trigger...

EPILOGUE

Federal agents had the church surrounded, waiting for Mox to come out. After the shot went off, they stormed the church, and in the mix of it all, Priscilla, Cleo and Tyrell were taken into custody. Authorities were never able to locate Mox.

-VALHALLAH CORRECTIONAL FACILITY-

"Yo Rell, tell the C.O. to crack my gate!" An inmate yelled.

"He ain't gon' do it unless you signed up for sick call." Tyrell replied.

"You the trustee, make it happen!"

"I don't even fuck wit' you like that, homey." Tyrell continued mopping the tier floor.

The C.O. shouted from inside the bubble. "Cell twenty-one! Daniels! Sick call!"

Tyrell dropped the mop he was holding, waited until he heard the cell door open, and then he started walking down the tier. He dug his hand inside his sweatpants and fetched his prison gun. When he reached the front of cell twenty-one, the inmate had just stepped out. Tyrell gripped the handmade shank in his palm, bit down on his lip and approached the inmate. "I got a gift from Mox," he said, shoving the sharpened tip of the shank into the target's abdomen. He pulled it out and stuck it in his chest directly over his heart and blood squirted from the hole and splashed his t-shirt.

Cleo pulled the shank out of his chest and the blood poured out even faster. On his way to the floor, he looked up and all he saw was Tyrell's back as he slowly walked off.

SUMMER 2013

Illuminant rays burst out the sun, giving the sky a bright yellowish tint. Not a cloud was in sight as the children played amongst themselves on swings, monkey bars, and in the sandbox. Parents and siblings sat on benches and stood against fences watching their little ones have the time of their life.

Ms. Davis sat on the bench she usually sat on when she brought her granddaughter to the park. It was the shadiest area of the playground, and she could see the entire park from her sitting position. With her newspaper in hand, she skimmed through the day's topics searching for something interesting to read.

"Crime, crime and more crime." She mumbled to herself, flipping through the pages. A droplet of water landed on her arm and she looked around to see if one of the kids was playing with a water gun, but she hadn't spotted any. Suddenly, another droplet hit her and then three more. When she looked up she saw dark clouds forming in the sky, and before she knew it, thunder was roaring and lighting struck down from the heavens above.

Parents scurried to find their children, grabbing them up, rushing to their vehicles before the torrential rains fell.

Ms. Davis stood up and walked over to the swings where she had last seen Brandi. "Brandi!" she called. "Brandi, where are you?"

Jasmine kept her foot on the brake with the car in drive. "Hurry up, c'mon!"

"Where we going, Daddy?" Brandi asked, holding onto Mox's hand as tight as she could as they ran to the waiting car.

"We goin' home, baby... we goin' home..."

-THE END-

CPSIA information can be obtained at www.ICGtesting.com
Printed in the USA
LVOW06s2349070314

376490LV00032B/932/P